THE SUPER GIRL SEVEN

To Blue,
Best Wishes

J. P. Olsen

THE SUPER GIRL SEVEN

T.P. CLEMENTS

BROWN
DOG
BOOKS

Published under licence by Brown Dog Books and
The Self Publishing Partnership
7 Green Park Station, Bath BA1 1JB

www.selfpublishingpartnership.co.uk

ISBN printed book: 978-1-78545-277-2
ISBN e-book: 978-1-78545-278-9

Contents

CHAPTER I

Prelude

The creature sped forth through a discontented night's sky towards a bead of light far in the distance. Over hill and down dale it continued, flying just shy of the tops of the trees. Across the cold, still lake, unfettered by even the slightest breeze it coursed on silently until rising sharply towards its beacon. Behind the window from which the light emanated, Portia Forbes Hamilton lay in her bed twisting and writhing helplessly until she was awoken by a dull thud outside.

Sitting bolt upright in response to it, her chest heaving, and brow beaded with sweat, she paused momentarily before casting her bed linen aside and making straight for the window. Her warm breath misted the small individual panes of the leaded light glass as she peered into the empty but foreboding darkness.

"Nothing," she uttered, as disappointed as she was relieved, "always nothing."

Taking a deep, calming breath, Portia returned to the sanctuary of her large four poster bed, drawing shut the thick, blood red velvet curtains which hung from it.

Ten thousand miles away, Marion Astley was reconciling herself to the imminent and bitter prospect of leaving her native Australia with her mother and five-year-old brother, Michael. As she stood on the deck of the huge passenger liner that was to take them to

England, she fought back tears gathering around her warm, hazel coloured eyes. The memory of her deceased father filled every thought in her head, and the love he had for his family, every picture in her mind's eye. Marion's brother was too young to feel the loss quite as she did, and ran around the deck in anticipation of an adventure. Leaning against the ship's railings, she felt the warmth of her mother's hand wrap around her wrist like a vine, drawing her closer.

"Come child," she said softly, "we must be strong, it's what your father would have wanted."

Marion looked upon her mother's face, her beautiful mother's face, now etched with the loss of the only man she had ever loved, but she kept her pain in so that Marion wouldn't break. Marion did the same so that her mother wouldn't either. The ship's funnel sounded, extinguishing the crippling silence between them as the hull began gently parting the water beneath it.

The morning sun broke Portia's slumbers, declaring itself through the very window she had fogged with panicked breath only hours before.

There was a knock at the door.

"Portia, do hurry up my darling," cried her mother, Madeline.

"You can come in mother," Portia cried across the vast expanse that was her bedroom.

"Always formality and etiquette in this family," she muttered disdainfully whilst reluctantly pulling herself up to a sitting position.

After a mere ten minutes, she was bolting across the grand reception area of her home, out through one of its great wooden doors and into the car awaiting her. Bidding Peter, the chauffeur, good morning, Portia sat back in the comfortable leather seats, wishing only she could walk the short distance to school like other mortals.

Because Portia's father, Horatio Forbes Hamilton, was the wealthiest and most influential man for many a mile, she could not live as others did.

Being prosperous had its advantages of course, but at twelve going on thirteen, Portia felt the burden of being groomed to take over as sole heir to her family's vast fortune. A few minutes later the car pulled into the driveway of the exclusive West Denton Public School, where she and other children of privilege from far and wide were educated. Portia, sensible that she was almost late, rushed from the car and up the stone stairs of the school's grand entrance; not dissimilar to the one she had hurried from only minutes before.

This was the third time in as many weeks she had narrowly avoided being late and each time it was her nightmares that had been causal, starving her of proper rest.

The day wore on. Portia limped through Latin, meandered through Greek Mythology and just when her eyelids were too heavy to keep from closing in French class, Mr. Forsyth the Headmaster knocked at the door.

Beckoning the class teacher, Mademoiselle Michelle, over, he spoke to her in hushed tone through the partially opened door without setting foot across the threshold. Once he had left, Mademoiselle Michelle walked over to where Portia was sitting and whispered in her ear. Portia was required to see the Headmaster in his study immediately, but why? As she made for the door, Portia searched her mind for any possible reason but could come up with nothing. She had been tired but to date this had not affected her work, and though she'd narrowly avoided being late on a number of occasions, she had yet to be. The heels of Portia's shoes resonated on the old, polished, wooden floors as she hurriedly made her way to Mr. Forsyth's office in the hope of securing an answer. Arriving at his study door at the end of a dark wood panelled corridor, Portia straightened her blazer with the palms of her hands and slightly tightened the knot in her tie. She gave a short sharp knock to convey an air of confidence.

"*Come!*" was the very brief and very quick response from within.

Portia gingerly opened the door to find Mr. Forsyth standing behind his desk with his back to it. He was staring through the leaded light windows over the institution he governed, his arms behind his back. Without seeing his face, one could almost surmise his expression was smug and self satisfied. Portia entered the room, whereupon Mr. Forsyth turned; the reflection from the light above passed over his glasses, obscuring any clear view of his eyes behind them.

"Ah," he began, almost as though he hadn't been expecting her.

"Miss Forbes Hamilton," he resumed, "please, sit down."

Portia seated herself; Mr. Forsyth remained standing.

There was a brief pause, wherein he seemed as if he were practising a speech in his head before speaking his words aloud. Then spreading out the fingers of both hands and pressing the tips together just beneath his chin, he began.

"Miss Forbes Hamilton, as you may or may not know we have recently had a reporter from London in our little village."

There followed a brief but uncomfortable silence, in which Mr. Forsyth searched Portia's face for a reaction.

"Yes," she replied after some moments "I had heard something."

"Then you may know that this gentleman was here to investigate this silly curse business," he continued dismissively.

"Yes Sir," replied Portia without delay, anxious there not be a reoccurrence of the previous awkwardness.

"Well it would seem this story has captured the public's imagination," resumed Mr. Forsyth, rocking his hands back and forth in the position he had kept them in.

"I myself do not believe in all this nonsense, but others do. Given these old folk legends involve your family, the board of trustees has become quite concerned," the gravity of his statement, he emphasized by leaning closer in and lowering his voice towards the end of it.

You see this school is one of the most prestigious in the country, indeed, the world. If people thought we had witches running around, attendance would tumble and pretty soon the institution would fall into financial ruin."

At the sound of this Portia's eyes narrowed and the blood rose in her cheeks.

Mr. Forsyth was clearly discomposed by this and gave a nervous cough before venturing to speak again.

Portia seized the opportunity it presented.

"Is this what you believe, that I am a witch?"

"Of course not," he protested, his complexion mirroring Portia's.

"Then what?" she asked coolly.

"It's not important what I think," stammered Mr. Forsyth.

"It is however, my job to keep everybody happy."

There was a brief silence, both parties rallying after the exchange.

"Do you not think that my having to deliver this decision hasn't given me many a moment's anguish?" he appealed.

Portia's face stiffened.

"Then it is decided Sir?" she asked rhetorically.

Mr. Forsyth exhaled despairingly.

"Yes, it has been decided," he conceded.

"Where am I to go?" asked Portia, suddenly feeling orphaned.

"The Sir Frederick Stanley."

"*The Stanley!*" Portia blurted in disbelief, "a citadel for the poor but gifted! I am not poor," protested Portia angrily.

"And you are not gifted," Mr. Forsyth quickly shot back.

Portia's face turned crimson, for as clever as she was and as hard as she tried, she knew in her heart, he was right.

"You see," he resumed, "this is an opportunity in disguise. All the money and influence your family has wouldn't normally be enough to secure you a place at The Sir Frederick Stanley. However, a situation has arisen, whereby…" he paused, his eyes narrowing behind his round spectacles.

"Let us say that a mutually beneficial swap can take place. To be frank Miss Forbes Hamilton, they do better over there than we do here. Of course," he added, his tone quite serious, "I would deny saying such a thing, should our conversation be repeated."

Portia sat in stunned silence; the thought of being dismissed from the school she was born to attend was more than she could bear. Added to which, her father was one of its most generous benefactors.

"What has my father to say of this?" she asked pointedly.

Mr. Forsyth's expression softened at this enquiry.

"He had the final decision in the matter," he replied, clearly unburdening himself of a measure of blame.

Moments passed without a word from either party. Portia sat gazing at the floor, her head heavy with a crown of disappointment. A paper passed before her eyes, held between Mr. Forsyth's thumb and forefinger.

"Here take this," he said in a conciliatory tone.

Portia took the paper by way of reflex, having no idea what was printed upon it.

"What is it?" she asked.

"It's a letter the Sir Fredrick Stanley School sends out to the few who are lucky enough to attend. You see Miss..." Mr. Forsyth paused, before resuming.

"You see Portia, this really is an opportunity for you, an opportunity to receive an even better education than we can give you here."

Portia looked at him searchingly.

"Not least though," he continued, "an opportunity to escape from gossip and all this silly talk of witches and the curse."

There was an uncomfortable silence that hung in the air.

"Will that be all?" Portia enquired boldly, anticipating her dismissal.

"Yes, that will be all," replied Mr. Forsyth, forcing a scant smile on a guilt-ridden face.

Portia rose from her chair, placing it quietly back in the position she had found it and made for the door.

Pulling it open, she was halted by the sound of Mr. Forsyth's voice.

"Good luck Miss Forbes Hamilton," he said rather timorously.

Portia turned, casting a stony expression upon him.

"Thank you, Sir," she said simply, before turning to complete her exit.

As soon as she was on the other side of the door, Portia rushed through the building to the nearest exit and out into the courtyard. School was over for the day and the building was empty save a few teachers and stragglers.

Not remembering Peter would be waiting to pick her up as he always did, Portia sought solace on some steps behind a wall in the school grounds.

There she sat for some moments, wondering had she acted differently would it have influenced the decision to dismiss her.

Fraught with anxiety and an overbearing sense of failure, she held up the letter Mr. Forsyth had handed her and began to read it.

Welcome to the Sir Frederick Stanley School for Girls and Boys.

Situated in the town of Sutton Althorpe, the school was founded in 1869 by Sir Frederick Stanley, a local steel baron.

He himself had been poorly educated but had a keen mind and rose through the ranks of Britain's industrialists. Towards the end of his life he and his wife, Ophelia Stanley, generously bequeathed one of their stately homes to be converted into a school. Their wish was that no gifted child be overlooked because of their lack of social status.

Over the last 100 years the Stanley has done just that, educating children from far and wide who otherwise might not have had the chance. The Stanley boasts opportunities for the academic, artistic and athletic.

Set in the beautiful English countryside, the school grounds sprawl onto the border of neighbouring town, West Denton.

If you are reading this letter it is probably because you have been accepted into The Sir Frederick Stanley. The school where magic happens.

As the last words fell from Marion's lips, the paper she was holding flapped in the wind that whipped around the deck of the boat.

"Feel any better?" asked her mother, kindly.

"A little," she replied.

"Your father would have been so very proud."

"Yes mother," was the only reply Marion was sure would not result in her bursting into tears.

"Come child, bring your brother and let's go in, it's getting cold."

Marion corralled Michael and the three of them made for their cabin as the ship forged on through the night.

After school Portia took a walk in the grounds of the estate to think upon the day's events. It was Friday, two clear days before she was to set foot in the Sir Frederick Stanley. Had her father not supported the decision to have her removed from The West Denton School, she would have felt guiltier. As it was, all Portia felt was confused, that and apprehensive about mixing with people at her new school she had no experience of, *'the ordinary people'*.

Afternoon was giving way to evening, evidenced by a flock of Jackdaws that flew noisily overhead towards a stand of skeletal, old oak trees. Portia decided to head home before the evening betrayed her to the night. It had been wet over the last few days and the ground had become sodden. She made slow progress and was hampered further by improper footwear. Portia had ventured out on a whim and not thought to change out of her school uniform. The clouds thickened overhead and soon mercilessly rang themselves out on whomever and whatever was beneath them.

Portia hastened her pace but the sodden ground beneath her low-heeled shoes sucked the life out of every stride she made. The rain began to come down harder and faster until it almost completely erased the outline of her house way in the distance. Cantering down a grassy bank that had become muddy with the recent wet weather, Portia gathered speed so she may scramble up its opposite incline. Nearing the top, she lost her footing and tumbled back down from whence she came. Covered in mud, tired and cold, Portia immediately tried to raise herself, but could not. She had fallen awkwardly, twisted her ankle and found upon inspection it was swelling rapidly.

Nights were harsh in this part of England and the terrain unforgiving. There was little chance of being eaten by a beast but every chance of dying of the cold. Portia knew not to panic and immediately began to look around for a branch that may serve as a crutch but could find nothing suitable. The rain suddenly stopped, quickly replaced by a thickening mist. Portia entertained, albeit briefly, the possibility of dragging herself the mile or so home, however, there was a stream to cross and a hill to ascend. She began to shiver with the cold and wrapped her arms around herself so she might not. 'Imagine,' she thought, 'expiring a mile away from home in the grounds of your parents' estate; to say nothing of being dismissed from the school that you were born to attend, what would they think?'

Portia thought hard whilst peeling back her wet sock to check on her injury. She tried once again to stand on her swollen, almost unrecognisable ankle but no sooner had she, than a sharp pain shot through her body sending her back to the ground. The dark clouds that had filled the sky only half an hour ago were now rapidly being painted over by the onset of darkness. Portia felt a sense of hopelessness wash over her and shook herself so she did not acquiesce to it. "*Think!*" she growled aloud, whilst silently admonishing herself for the present situation she was in. Time passed, the temperature dropped further, Portia began to waiver in and out of consciousness. She drifted asleep momentarily but was soon awoken by a dull, flapping sound close by. Her eyes widened as she scoured the near dark for the source of it. She could see nothing at first, but kept looking, feeling that someone or something's eyes were upon her. Concluding she had imagined hearing something out of desperation, Portia sank back with conflicting feelings of relief and despair. As she slipped gently into unconsciousness, she was awoken abruptly again by a loud cawing sound. This, thought Portia, too loud and too clear to be the product of any unconscious wandering. She was right too, for up in one of the old, bare, oak trees, perched a very large bird.

Uncertain of the species, Portia was inclined to think it a Raven. Looking at it as intently as she could in the very last light yet to be stolen by darkness, she felt it staring back at her. For a moment, their eyes were locked upon each other, until all of a sudden Portia saw herself from the bird's perspective. So real was the image in fact, that for a fleeting moment she imagined she had died and left her own body. Letting out a muzzled scream, Portia sank back into unconsciousness; the cold, wet, muddy hollow seemingly her final resting place.

Minutes, hours, days later, unaware how much time had passed, or not as the case maybe, Portia imagined herself awake.

Geoffrey, the faithful, family butler appeared to be sitting cross legged in an armchair beside her bed.

She opened her eyes wider and remembered the horrifying view of herself lying at the foot of the hill. Portia gasped, Geoffrey quickly rose to his feet and leaned around the thick velvet curtains gathered against the post of her bed. There was a brief silence as Portia looked upon Geoffrey's strong but kindly face.

"Are you dead too?" she asked, her eyes narrowing as she posed her question.

"No Miss Portia, we are neither of us dead," replied Geoffrey, his smile widening as he delivered the welcome but confusing news.

"Then what?" asked Portia, attempting to raise herself up to a seated position, until the pain from her ankle convinced her otherwise.

"You had a fall Miss Portia, a nasty one by all accounts, the doctor says you have fractured your ankle."

"But who found me?" Portia enquired with a puzzled expression.

"I did Miss."

"How?"

"Oh quite by chance Miss."

Portia looked at Geoffrey searchingly in order to secure a fuller explanation.

"Well since you will not rest without a complete account, I will tell you," replied Geoffrey with a smile.

"But only if you promise to stay lying down, you must get your rest Miss Portia."

Portia nodded a 'yes'.

"Very well," she added.

Geoffrey reclaimed his seat and began.

"The house was quiet; your mother and father were in the drawing room after having dined with some business associates. Since they did not need me for a little while and one of the other staff could take care of them, I decided to take Percival for a walk. The vet said he should get proper exercise after his injury, so it seemed an ideal time to take him for a stroll in the grounds. It had yet to start raining and we had not intended to go far, as you know he is not the most…" Geoffrey paused and smiled, "let us say boisterous of hounds."

Portia smiled back.

"However, almost as soon as we left the house he began to pull on his lead, all the time with his nose hard against the ground. Blood hounds will be blood hounds I thought to myself, but I had never seen Percival quite so determined.

I hurried as fast as conditions would allow, thinking perhaps there was an animal in distress or your father had poachers on his land. Eventually Percival broke free of my grip and chased down the hill to where you were lying. I caught up with him some minutes later to find you huddled in a ball, cold and unconscious." Geoffrey paused momentarily, losing for a fraction of a second, his trade mark composure.

Observing this, Portia allowed the moment to pass without comment.

"How did you get me home?" she then asked.

"Well Miss…" Geoffrey faltered, as if he was in danger of giving something away.

"You're home, that's the main thing."

"Please," implored Portia.

"I carried you Miss," he eventually conceded.

She gasped, raising her hand to her mouth.

"But that's over a mile, and in such conditions."

Geoffrey smiled an awkward smile.

"I could not have left you Miss Portia, much longer out there and you would have frozen to death."

There was an awkward silence in which Portia's eyes turned watery.

"You saved my life Geoffrey," she said with a failing voice.

He rose from his chair, clearly moved by her words.

Then laying the front of his tail coat flat with the palms of his hands, he made for the door.

"I'll let your parents know that you are awake," he said softly before leaving.

As he made his exit, his progress was halted by Portia's voice.

"Geoffrey," she called.

He turned to face her.

"Thank you."

Geoffrey gave a slight nod of his head, "Miss Portia," he replied before completely exiting the room.

CHAPTER 2

A New Beginning

Monday morning came around with unforgivable haste. With a little help from Peter, Portia clumsily made her way into the waiting car, crutches and all.

"There you are Miss Portia," he began, turning in his seat to address her, "now you have a legitimate reason to be driven to school." Peter smiled, the action of which pushed his boyish, rosy cheeks closer towards his clear, blue eyes. Returning to face the windscreen, he adjusted his cap over his curly, blonde hair and started the silver and black Bentley's engine. It was a little more of a drive to the Stanley than it was to Portia's previous school, though to her thinking they arrived all too quickly. She hobbled into its main building courtesy of her crutches with Peter following alongside, holding her satchel and books. Once she was settled, he left. Portia felt the full weight of his absence immediately he'd gone. She was alone in a school she never expected to attend and knew not a soul there.

Then to compound matters, she heard mention of a name that was bitterly familiar to her.

"*Oh Miss Hoskins!*" called a voice from deep within the hallway.

Portia winced at the very utterance of the name, not only because Miss Hoskins' reputation had earned her the title of, 'The Dragon Lady', but because she and the dragon lady had a shared history. Out of the darkness Miss Hoskins marched stiffly towards her. Portia decided she would try to lose herself in the crowd of girls and boys heading to their classes. She was however, exceptionally tall with blonde hair and presently getting about on crutches, not a particularly easy girl to miss. Ducking down as best she could to avoid detection, Portia made an awkward turn and headed in the opposite direction.

Just when she thought she had successfully evaded the dragon lady, she felt a hand on the back of her shoulder.

"Just the young lady," said a voice, the tone of which could only have belonged to a man.

Before she had time to turn, Mr. Bradley, the school's Headmaster appeared before her.

"My apologies," he began, "I fear I quite startled you," he added, observing the expression on Portia's face.

"Oh no Sir," she replied, her panicked tone suggesting otherwise.

As she had finished speaking, Miss Hoskins drew alongside the pair of them.

"Ah Miss Hoskins," said Mr. Bradley "have you met our new pupil, Miss Forbes Hamilton?"

The dragon lady stood before Portia, eyes narrowed, lips pursed and her shoulders back.

Behind her glasses, her eyes travelled from left to right purposefully.

Portia steeled herself against the cold, unsubtle scrutiny she was being subjected to.

The moment seemed to last an eternity.

"Well," she rasped "don't expect any special treatment here Miss Forbes Hamilton."

Then taking her leave of Mr. Bradley, she marched stiffly back from whence she came.

"Hmm," he muttered in the silence left to him, "don't mind Miss Hoskins, she's not much of a morning person. Then again, I hardly think she does better in the afternoon, evening or night," he added with a wry smile.

"Come, Miss Forbes Hamilton, I'll introduce you to your new teachers."

The next few days didn't yield many surprises, Portia had made no new friends, but on an optimistic note the school wasn't abound with stories of witches and curses. All in all, she'd made a good start, although she found the pupils in the school quite cliquey. To her surprise, they appeared every bit as exclusive as their wealthy counterparts. In the middle of her second week Portia found herself in a hurry between lessons. She had become very adept with her crutches, but evidently not as adept at holding on to her books and papers while she got around on them. Between one flight of stairs and another, Portia lost her grip on her school work, watching it cascade out of her hand and float lazily down into the stairwell. This would have been less of an ordeal if the teacher taking the next lesson wasn't the dragon lady herself. Miss Hoskins was known for the swift and harsh punishment of anything beyond drawing breath, being late for her lesson was unthinkable. Portia bit her lip nervously at the very thought of what seemed inevitable. As she made her way down the stairs, clumsily retrieving the few papers within her grasp, she heard the voices of other girls coming from below. They became louder until the three girls to whom they belonged appeared on the same flight of stairs Portia was precariously perched upon. They had in their hands what looked like the rest of her school work, 'but what?' thought Portia, 'were they going to do with it?' She had visions of them tearing it up and dropping it into the stairwell as confetti, or worse still, stealing her crutches and running off with them.

The brief silence that ensued was broken by the smallest of the girls. She held out her hand, tossing her long, dark, wavy hair from her face.

"Here," she said, "hand me the rest of your work."

Portia stiffened

"Why?" she asked, her tone peppered with suspicion.

The dark haired girl looked at her two friends, a fair haired girl who was to Portia's eye very plain, and a bright, blonde haired girl who was the exact opposite.

"So we can put your papers back in order, silly," beamed the dark haired girl.

"Come, quickly!" said the blonde haired girl, gesturing for Portia to hand over the remainder of her work.

Portia did as she was asked, *or commanded to do in her opinion*, resuming her descent whilst the other girls quickly reassembled her papers.

At the bottom of the stairs the three girls waited for her to catch up.

"*Hurry!*" said the dark haired girl, "there's a short cut through the boiler room."

"But...?" Portia protested.

"No time for that," said the blonde haired girl, placing her hand upon Portia's forearm and guiding her through a doorway. Moments later after negotiating the labyrinth that was the boiler room, Portia was lined up with the rest of the class awaiting the dreaded dragon lady. Just in time too, for she appeared only seconds later, her loud raspy voice announcing her arrival.

"Right!" she barked from the opposite end of the line, "everybody in, run, run, run, don't keep me waiting."

After lunch and before the afternoon lessons resumed, Portia sought out a quiet spot within the school grounds to read. Crossing the playground, she caught sight of the three girls who had saved her from the wrath of Miss Hoskins in the morning. Portia had yet to thank them for what they had done and knew it only proper to do so.

"I say," began Portia once she was closer to them. The three girls who had been facing away, turned around.

"Hello," said Portia awkwardly, smiling similarly.

"Hello," chimed the three girls.

There was a brief silence.

"I wanted to thank you for what you did for me," Portia resumed.

"Oh that's alright," replied the dark haired girl with a broad smile.

"Yes," interjected the blonde haired girl, "wouldn't want to get on the wrong side of the dragon lady this early in the school year."

"Or ever for that matter," giggled the first girl to speak.

"I'm Morwenna Morrison, Momo," she announced putting her hand out to shake Portia's.

Portia steadied her crutch between her arm and torso and shook Morwenna's waiting hand.

"Portia," she replied, "Portia Forbes Hamilton."

The blonde girl introduced herself next.

"Eliza Crofton, Solo."

Portia also shook her hand, her expression betraying she was noticing a pattern.

"Angela Murphy," announced the last girl, "Angel."

Portia shook her hand too, with a look of confusion now residing upon her face.

"Excuse me asking but why do you all have nick names?"

The three girls smiled in unison.

"They're our Super Girl names," offered Momo by way of an explanation.

"Your what, names?"

"Our Super Girl names," replied Momo.

Portia paused to consider her next question.

"What are the Super Girls?" she asked.

"Us," replied Solo.

"The gifted misfits," interjected Angel with a smile.

Portia's face fell as if she was hoping for a much grander explanation.

"You see," began Solo, "none of us started at the beginning of the school year like all the other kids, consequently we found it hard to make friends."

"You might have noticed it's very cliquey here," commented Angel.

"Yes I have," agreed Portia.

"So," said Momo, picking up from where Angel had left off, "we formed our own exclusive club."

"A sort of new girls' club if you will," said Solo.

"Exactly," chimed Momo and Angel.

Portia remained quiet, but very much wanted to ask if she could join.

She'd never had a large circle of friends and was an only child, added to which recent events at her old school had frightened most everybody away.

"You can join us if you like," said Momo smiling in a somewhat mischievous way.

"*Can I?*" replied Portia with more than a little enthusiasm.

27

"Yes of course," said Momo, her smile broadening.

"One thing though," remarked Angel.

Portia's face fell in anticipation of an impediment to her being one of the Super Girls.

"What is it?" she asked almost meekly.

"You have to have a Super Girl name," Solo pointed out.

An expression of relief passed over Portia's face.

"Ok," she replied allowing a little excitement to surface in her voice.

"But what?" mused Angel, pressing her finger to her lips.

There was a brief pause.

"*Willow!*" Momo announced enthusiastically.

"Why Willow?" asked Portia.

"Well because you're so tall and slender, like a willow tree. Don't you like it?" Momo asked, anticipating that she didn't.

Portia paused whilst Momo searched her face for an answer.

"I think Willow will do very well," she replied with a big grin.

"Then you're one of us now," said Solo taking up one of Willow's hands in hers.

CHAPTER 3

Then There Were Seven

"Finally!" exclaimed Marion, as the boat which she and her family had been travelling on for the past six weeks docked in Liverpool. Marion made her way down the iron stairs connecting it to dry land as quickly as the string of other passengers allowed, leaving her mother to chaperone her younger brother. 'Soon,' she thought, 'the boat would be returning to Australia, her home and final resting place of her father.' It was in this moment she felt the greatest detachment from him. Marion had hated it on the boat and felt somehow she was betraying her father by being on it. Now though, all she felt was she had betrayed him, that she had abandoned him. Her stomach churned, her throat tightened, and just when she felt she might lose her composure altogether, she heard a voice emanating from the sea of people swelling around her.

"I say… I say…" came the shrill strains from within it.

Marion looked about her trying to locate the sound, until she was engulfed by somebody or something in a mohair coat.

Momentarily the mohair coat released its grip, revealing Marion's eccentric aunt Mildred.

"There you are my little kangaroo," she bleated, pinching the little kangaroo's cheeks without any thoughts for its dignity.

Then in a flash the mohair coat took off down the dock towards

Marion's mother and brother who had by this time disembarked. Now it was their turn to be accosted.

Marion looked around her as the crowd of people began to disperse.

"So this is England," she said to herself, before beginning to sneeze violently and feel her face itch. Some moments later her mother, little brother and aunt Mildred came into sharp focus. Marion's mother wore an expression of concern.

"My dear!" she gasped, putting her hand to her lips, as if to stifle her consternation, "whatever's happened to your face?"

"What do you mean mother?" replied Marion between sneezes.

"Take a look dear," said aunt Mildred, hurriedly producing a small, compact mirror from her bag and handing it to her niece.

Marion opened it and gingerly brought it into her line of sight.

She gasped when her reflection revealed her face was covered in dark red spots about the size of a child's, small finger nail.

"Oh mother!" she exclaimed.

"Five minutes in England and I look like a circus freak, and I have to start a new school in three days."

"There, there dear," said her mother in a conciliatory tone, "I'm sure it will go down considerably by then."

"Yes dear," interjected aunt Mildred, "we have an excellent doctor in the village too, if it doesn't."

The party made their way to the transport that was to take them the remainder of their journey, with Marion sneezing the whole time.

The weekend vanished as if it were the subject of a conjuring trick. On Monday morning Marion found herself occupying the front passenger seat of the car whilst aunt Mildred drove her to school.

As it was her first day, her mother and brother accompanied them too. With the whole business of just arriving in England, the funny accents and the endless cups of tea, Marion had not yet turned her attentions to her new school. Now though, she had no choice, not least because aunt Mildred wouldn't stop talking for the entire journey, about how proud she was that Marion would be attending there. Once they had arrived, her aunt paused to look through the windscreen at the sight before her.

"Marvellous," she declared, "what an opportunity."

Then springing from the car as if she were Marion's age, she fussed and flapped until everyone had joined her.

She then positioned a hand on her hip, so Marion felt obliged to put hers through the gap it presented. Marion looked at her mother imploring her to distract her aunt. Having to come to a new school in a new country with a blotchy face was one thing, having your eccentric aunt chaperone you to the door, was entirely another.

"Come Mildred," said Marion's mother, "why don't you take me and Michael into town."

Marion seized her opportunity, kissed them all very quickly and ran as fast as she could in the direction of the school gates.

On Thursday evening at dinner, aunt Mildred enquired about her niece's progress at school.

"Well my little kangaroo," she began, "have you made any friends? I expect not, just yet," aunt Mildred answered her own question. "I hear they're terribly cliquey at that school."

"I have actually," replied Marion rather proudly.

"Oh!" exclaimed her aunt, "do tell."

"Yes," said Marion's mother leaning a little closer into her daughter.

"Well, I have made four friends really."

"Four indeed," commented aunt Mildred with a curious expression of surprise and disbelief.

"Yes auntie, four," Marion assured her.

"Who are these girls?" asked her mother, exhibiting a smile that Marion had not seen the likes of for many a week.

"They are all girls, aren't they?" interjected aunt Mildred, anxiously.

"Oh yes auntie, she sighed, "no boys."

"Very well," said aunt Mildred, her expression softening.

"Well, where was I?" resumed Marion.

"Oh yes, my new friends. Well they call themselves the Super Girls."

"The Super Girls?" repeated Marion's mother with a quizzical expression.

"Yes mother."

"Why so?"

"I don't really know. They're like a club for new girls. They all have nicknames too. There's Momo, Angel, Solo, Willow and now me."

"And what have they called you?"

"Roo, mother, short for Kangaroo."

"How interesting."

"What are these girls' real names?" asked aunt Mildred.

"Well let me see. Solo's real name is Eliza Crofton."

"That must be Maximilian Crofton the surgeon's daughter," commented aunt Mildred enthusiastically.

"You know this girl's father?" asked Marion's mother.

"It's a small town, Penelope, everybody knows everybody and everything about each other here. He's a very respectable man, dashing too. He came up from down south a couple of months ago. I hear he's a bit of a maverick, a loose cannon if you will. They say he had some trouble at the hospital he previously worked at.

Whose next Marion?" asked aunt Mildred, clearly engaged in her favourite pastime, gossip.

"Angel, Angela Murphy," replied Marion.

"Ah, Glenda and Alan's daughter, they run a grocer's shop in Sutton Althorpe.

"A nice family, steady people," concluded aunt Mildred, almost as if disappointed this was the case.

"Next?" she asked with great anticipation.

"Momo, Morwenna Morrison,"

"The Morrisons, lovely people, queer mix of a doctor and cabinet maker, still, they seem to get along. Their daughter Morwenna's a sterling sort of girl too, always has a smile on her face. One more?" said aunt Mildred, leaning a little across the table, her face all expectation.

"Portia Hamilton Forbes... no wait," giggled Marion, "Portia Forbes Hamilton, yes that's her name, we call her Willow though."

At the sound of this name aunt Mildred slowly recoiled and her complexion turned pale.

"The Forbes Hamilton girl?" she repeated through narrowed eyes, her tone slow and deliberate.

"Yes, that's right," Marion confirmed, sensing all too easily that something was awry.

"What is it that concerns you about this particular girl Mildred?" Penelope enquired, feeling the same ill ease as her daughter.

"Simply that those with reputations built on infamy should be avoided at all costs."

"Infamy!" gasped Marion's mother; *"criminal conduct?!"*

"No Penelope," replied aunt Mildred shaking her head solemnly, "far worse than that."

33

THE SUPER GIRL SEVEN

"What could possibly be worse than that?"

There was a brief pause.

Marion and her mother sat agog, waiting for aunt Mildred's reply.

"Black magic," were the words that finally escaped her lips.

"The occult?!"

"Yes dear, the occult!"

"What exactly do you mean?"

"Well Penelope," aunt Mildred continued, "it's said and believed by most, that the village is cursed and has been for over a century. Nobody seems to be in possession of all the facts, but the Forbes Hamilton's are thought to be at the centre of it. They own most of the neighbouring village, including Horseforth Manor. That's where it's said most of the trouble started and the reason the family gave it away to be used as a museum. We recently had a reporter up from London to investigate the whole terrible business, two weeks later the Forbes Hamilton girl turns up at the Stanley because her own school won't have her anymore.

"How much evidence is there to support such outrageous claims?" asked Marion's mother, always much slower to judge than most mortals and ever the voice of reason.

"Look over the town's history in the parish records when you get a chance, or through old newspapers in the library.

It's all there, mining accidents, freak floods, why even a passenger plane fell out of the sky onto the village a few years back."

"But those accidents could have happened anywhere Mildred," reasoned Marion's mother.

"But they didn't Penelope, they happened here in Sutton Althorpe, where they always do."

There was an awkward pause, broken by the sound of aunt Mildred pushing her chair away from the table causing the legs to scrape on the floor.

Getting up, she sighed despondently.

"I'm going to take Satch for a walk," she added resignedly.

Making for the door she cast an intently serious expression Marion's way.

"Be very careful mixing with the likes of the Forbes Hamilton's my dear," she warned.

Then with one quick, "see you both later," she crossed the kitchen calling for Satch, her black and white border collie.

Marion and her mother remained silent for some moments, only a bemused expression passed between them.

"What do you make of that mother?" asked Marion in a perplexed tone.

"Oh your aunt Mildred has always been a little on the superstitious side."

"Do you think I should avoid the Forbes Hamilton girl? I mean, do you think any of that business aunt Mildred spoke of is true?"

"I think your aunt is trying to protect you, and that this is her way of doing it."

"So the rumours could have some truth to them?" Marion pressed.

"I imagine small town people in England are not dissimilar to small town people in Australia, they just have more history here to embroider a story with.

You must make your own decision about this girl as you would any other person, based upon her actions and not hearsay. Now," she continued, "let's go and check on Michael, he's being altogether too quiet upstairs and we both know that can only mean he's up to mischief."

Over the weeks that followed, Roo (as she was getting used to being called) formed a very close attachment to the rest of the Super Girls. They had become like another family to her. Although she kept a wary eye on Willow, her aunt's suspicions were never substantiated. At most, Willow was sometimes a little distant, usually haughty and occasionally awkward, not classic behaviour for someone who was supposed to be a witch. If anything, Willow was a good shepherd, and had for this reason fallen into the role of leader. At the end of one lunch time, she, Roo and Angel were making their way to their next lesson. On their way, they heard the voices of other pupils' coming from behind a walled area of the school's grounds.

"Looks like a bumble bee to me," said a boy's voice.

"Yeah, or a wasp," said another.

Willow immediately drew to a halt so she could listen more carefully.

Again, the same comments were being made, but this time they were accompanied by loud 'buzzing' sorts of sounds.

"Come," said Willow to the other two girls, making haste to where the voices were emanating from.

As she rounded one of the walls, Willow was met by three boys all of whom were a couple of years older than she. Behind them and somewhat obscured stood a girl who was either very small for her age, or was about ten years old by Willow's estimation. The long, dark haired, little girl was dressed in a fairly worn calf length skirt, a fluffy yellow and black hooped sweater and black shoes that had evidently seen much wear. Seeing that the boys were obviously ridiculing the diminutive stranger, Willow wasted no time, barging by them to her aid, Roo and Angel quickly followed.

"Have you nothing better to do, you pond slime?" Willow demanded of the boys. The boys were caught off guard and discomposed by Willow's searing description of them. Willow could do that to a person, she had a way about her.

"Well?" she demanded, her tone defying any witty or scathing retort the 'pond slime' might have been considering.

The three boys turned, mumbling under their breath as they left.

"Witch," they shouted once out of sight.

For an almost imperceptible moment Willow was caught off guard. 'There it was', thought Roo to herself, the chink in Willow's seemingly impenetrable armour, and all because someone had uttered the word, witch. Willow bent down to speak with the little girl, for there was at least eight inches difference in their height.

"Are you lost?" she asked in a soft, much less haughty voice than she usually spoke in.

"No," replied the little girl.

"Well, I took a wrong turn and ended up in the quadrangle, but I'm meant to be at the school."

"You are not from around here, are you?" asked Willow, who immediately caught the girls accent, identifying it as being Irish.

"No, I'm from Ireland, Belfast to be accurate."

"What's your name?" asked Willow.

"Anna, Anna McNamara."

Before Willow had time to introduce herself and the other girls, she was interrupted by a bell ringing for the next lesson.

"Time to go," she remarked, "who is your next lesson with?"

"Miss Hoskins," Anna replied.

"Quickly then," said Willow, "put your blazer back on and come with us. Did no one tell you that you are not to remove it in school?"

Anna blushed, a look of helplessness spread across her face.

"I don't have a blazer," she replied.

Willow's face pinched with curiosity, as did Roo and Angel's.

"What do you mean, you don't have a blazer?"

"It's a long story," replied Anna with a forlorn expression.

Willow looked at Roo and Angel.

"Miss Hoskins will skin her alive if she goes into class dressed like that," she commented.

"That's for sure," agreed Roo. "I have an idea!" she exclaimed, her face brightening with sudden inspiration.

"I'll give her mine."

"It's a nice thought Roo," said Willow, "better she takes mine though."

"'But then you'll get in trouble and Miss Hoskins already hates you."

"Precisely," agreed Willow, "nothing I do, good or bad, will alter her opinion of me, you on the other hand have yet to fall foul of her."

Roo looked at Willow, who was already slipping her long slender arms out of her blazer, "give it time," she said with a wink.

Smiling, she helped Anna on with her jacket and hurriedly ushered her away, with Roo and Angel at her side.

Presently the four of them were lined up outside Miss Hoskins' class, where they waited with trepidation for her arrival. Willow stood flushed from running, in her crisp, white blouse but no blazer. Beside her, Anna stood drowning in a blazer so long, it took on the look of a dress. Willow gestured to her to roll up the sleeves of the woefully ill-fitting garment. Suddenly the heavy, matronly steps of Miss Hoskins could be heard resonating throughout the corridor. Presently she stood before her class. Willow felt sure Miss Hoskins had observed she was not properly attired but had chosen to temporarily ignore it. Instead she looked down at her class register, which she carried around on a clipboard.

"Anna McNamara, show yourself girl," she scowled, "as if it's not obvious," she added with a sarcastic grin.

Anna sheepishly raised her hand.

"Well girl," Miss Hoskins spat, "come here, don't expect me to come to you.

We can't all have servants, can we?" she rasped, looking directly at Willow.

Anna slowly made her way to the front of the line, clearly fearful of the outcome.

Once there, Miss Hoskins looked her up and down as if she had crawled out of a rotten apple and then waved her lazily into the classroom.

"Oh one thing," she said after Anna had taken only a few steps.

"Have a proper school uniform on tomorrow or don't come back until you do,"

'Please don't answer her back,' was the only thought that entered Willow's head and doubtless any other pupil in the class who had a heart.

Anna turned to respond.

'This could go either way,' thought Willow, as she looked on, nervously.

"Yes Miss," replied Anna to the relief of all except Miss Hoskins, who loved any opportunity to reprimand or berate, no matter how tenuous the reason.

The rest of the pupils filed into class on her command; Miss Hoskins' arm, falling like a guillotine when Willow reached the threshold.

"Not you Miss Forbes Hamilton," she said with a cold, self-satisfied grin.

There was an awkward pause, for she always liked to watch her prey squirm. Portia steeled herself against Miss Hoskins' inevitable wrath and subsequent punishment. However just as she was about to unleash her tirade, Mr. Bradley turned up as if a genie had granted Willow a wish.

He wore a perplexed expression on his face. Anxious to rid himself of it he ventured to speak.

"Miss Hoskins, what is the meaning of this, pupils running around the school without proper uniform?"

"I was about to take care of it," she replied, barely able to stifle her glee.

"Miss Forbes Hamilton, do you have any good reason why you are not wearing your blazer?" asked Mr. Bradley.

"I'll take care of her Mr. Bradley," interrupted Miss Hoskins, anxious that the opportunity not slip from her grasp.

"Well, Miss Forbes Hamilton?" he persisted impatiently.

A silence ensued.

"I do not Sir," Willow finally replied, not wishing to betray Anna.

Roo and Angel looked on in silence, preserving Willow's ruse. Unable to keep quiet any longer, Roo stood up from her chair, the sound it made, amplified by the silence it intruded upon.

All eyes immediately turned towards her, including those made of granite, belonging to Miss Hoskins.

"Portia gave her jacket to the new girl Sir, she doesn't have one just yet and some of the older boys were making fun of her in the quadrangle because of it... Sir."

Mr. Bradley turned his attentions to Willow; Miss Hoskins' remained momentarily on Roo.

"Is this true Miss Forbes Hamilton?"

"Yes Sir," she reluctantly admitted.

Mr. Bradley stood with a pensive expression, until a broad smile beset his ruddy, moustached face.

"Excellent Miss Forbes Hamilton!" he exclaimed enthusiastically.

"Exactly what this school stands for, sticking up for the little man, or girl in this case," he chuckled.

Miss Hoskins' face went through various shades of red, until it resolved on a nice plum colour. To add insult to injury Mr. Bradley congratulated her for instilling such high morals in her pupils. Further compounding the dragon lady's humiliation, Willow was allowed to go home early so she didn't wander the school improperly dressed.

Later that evening there was a knock at the door of the house Anna and her family lived in.

"I'll go," she said

"Mind you see who it is first," her father warned her.

"I will," she hollered back.

Anna rumbled down the old, wooden staircase and peered through the mottled coloured glass window at the top of the door as she approached it.

The vague outline of the head and shoulders of a tall, dark haired man could be seen through it.

"Who is it?" Anna asked as she bent down, pushing the waist high letterbox open to take a look.

"Parcels for Miss Anna McNamara," said the man on the other side of the door in a cheery sort of way.

"There must be a mistake."

There was a brief pause, whilst the delivery man checked the address.

"No mistake," he informed her.

"Says here, Miss Anna McNamara, 71 Century Street, Sutton Althorpe."

Just as he had finished speaking Anna gingerly opened the door.

"Miss," he said, nodding over a pyramid of parcels; one round box in his hands, what appeared to be a shoebox on top of that, and a large neatly wrapped bundle on top of them both.

"Hello," Anna greeted him nervously.

"Well," enquired the man after some moments of silence, "aren't you going to take them?"

"What's in them?" asked Anna with a suspicious expression.

"Don't know Miss, only my job to deliver them, this one feels soft though," he said nodding towards the wrapped bundle.

"Certainly not ticking," he laughed, tilting his head as if to take a listen. At this, Anna bolted for the stairs, leaving the man on the step behind the partially opened door.

"Just kidding Miss," he shouted through the gap in an effort to alleviate Anna's inexplicable panic.

Anna halted, suddenly regaining her senses.

She turned, slowly retracing her steps back to him.

"You're not from around here are you Miss?" he asked with an enquiring look on his face.

"No," Anna replied, "I'm from Ireland, Belfast to be exact."

"I see," he replied thoughtfully. "It's terrible what's started to happen over there," he commented in a sympathetic tone.

"Yes it is," replied Anna sorrowfully.

There was a momentary silence.

"Well," he said, his face brightening, "you'll be quite safe here Miss, nothing like that happens in Sutton Althorpe. Nothing much of anything happens here come to think of it," he added.

"Not unless you believe in witches and curses," he joked, chuckling to himself.

"Welcome to the village Miss and good luck," he continued, handing over the parcels.

"Goodbye Miss," he said in parting, touching his cap before turning to leave.

"Goodbye and thank you," Anna replied.

Placing the parcels down carefully, which were rather heavier and bigger than they looked against the backdrop of the large framed delivery man, she paused to guess what was inside. Finally, after pinching, shaking and turning the package and boxes for some minutes, Anna could contain herself no longer. She carefully removed the string that encircled the soft package and then began to work the sticky tape free from the brown paper wrapping. The unmistakable smell of new fabric arose shortly before Anna exposed the beautiful midnight blue blazer within, the breast pocket of which was proudly emblazoned with the Sir Frederick Stanley School crest. Stitched into the lining behind the crest was the manufacturer's label; Anna read it aloud.

"Made in Scotland by Robert Galloway & Company, Finest Shetland Wool."

Under the blazer lay a red and green, tartan skirt with a blue background, made by the same manufacturer. Behind them both was the purest white cotton blouse Anna had ever seen in her life.

She turned her attention to the oblong box resting upon its circular counterpart.

Inside of that was a beautiful pair of patent leather, low heeled, shoes, exactly her size. Lastly, Anna opened the circular box, within which was a straw boater hat, around it, a band the same colour as the blazer.

'Who could have sent such wonderful things?' Anna thought to herself, 'and why?'

Now she would be able to attend school and not be taunted with names like wasp or bumble bee ever again. Anna carefully collected all the garments together and ran upstairs dizzy with excitement.

When an opportunity presented itself the next day at school, Anna made straight for where the Super Girls had congregated. Before she had time to speak, Willow spotted her.

"Much better," she announced kindly.

"I still have your blazer," Anna blurted out awkwardly.

"Not to worry, time for both of us to make a fresh start," replied Willow, touching her blazer at the cuff to emphasize she too had a new uniform.

"So Anna, what brings you to the Stanley?" enquired Solo.

"My parents moved all of us; I mean my three younger brothers and sister,"

Anna replied in a shy and sorrowful tone.

Sensing that Anna was being guarded and did not want to convey anymore details of her arrival, Willow tactfully altered the course of the conversation.

"Well, you can join us if you like."

"Can I?"

"Of course," interjected Momo. "You can be a Super Girl too."

"A what girl?" asked Anna with a confused look on her face.

"A Super Girl," repeated Momo.

"Oh," replied Anna, her expression fixed.

"You see, we are the gifted misfits," began Solo.

"Cast aside by the rest of the school population," said Momo in a very dramatic fashion as if she were performing in a Greek Tragedy.

Willow rolled her eyes playfully.

"We all came here after the school year had begun.

Momo and Angel were the only two of us who started on the same day," continued Willow. "It was difficult to make friends by then, so we started our own club, if you will."

Anna's eyes lit up at the thought of making five new friends on only her second day at school.

"Momo's a very unusual name," she commented

"It's my Super Girl name," giggled Momo.

"We all have a Super Girl name, that's the only rule."

"That, and you have to befriend any new girl who didn't start school at the beginning of the year," said Roo.

"Sound good?" asked Willow of Anna.

"Oh yes," she replied enthusiastically.

"Then we must find you a name," said Roo.

"Hmm," muttered Willow.

"Does anybody have any suggestions?" she asked the rest of the Super Girls.

The next few moments were filled with nonsensical mumbling.

Willow cast her eyes upon Anna, with a wry sort of expression on her face.

Anna looked at her quizzically, almost as if she knew what Willow was thinking.

Moments passed before Anna's quizzical expression turned into a smile, a smile that could calm the angriest of souls if it had to.

"Not wasp?" she giggled.

"It is far easier to say than bumble bee," laughed Willow.

"Besides it seems to suit you, and it shows the wretched pond slime didn't get to you, it is a statement," concluded Willow.

"Alright then," agreed Anna, "Wasp it is."

Over the next couple of months Wasp became firmly ensconced into the sisterhood that was the Super Girls. Still the memories of having her house burnt to the ground by terrorists during the onset of violence in her native Belfast haunted her. Still she remembered racing through a house billowing thick, black smoke in the middle of the night, only to find the doors had been barricaded from the outside. The lengths hatred could go to, Wasp found hard to comprehend, but here in the sleepy little village of Sutton Althorpe she felt safe.

The last few weeks of the school year were quickly evaporating. The Super Girls looked forward to spending the whole summer together, for as unlikely as it seemed they had melded into one unit. Six girls all from different walks of life that circumstances had swept together. It was then Bailey Barnes bounded onto the scene, for she couldn't just simply arrive like other girls. Bailey became acquainted with people very quickly, though because she was so loud and talkative she didn't make friends of most of them. After only days she had annoyed almost every pupil in the school except the Super Girls, who she had yet to meet. Whilst she skulked pitifully around the playground one day, four of them engaged her in conversation.

"Are you Bailey Barnes?" asked Roo in her forthright manner.

Bailey looked up, as if piqued by even such a simple question.

"That's right," she replied, her tone and expression equally suspicious.

"And you are?" she returned indignantly.

Roo paused to look at the other Super Girls.

"I'm Roo," she said, with a proud grin on her face.

"Who?" asked Bailey looking quizzically at her.

"Roo," repeated Roo.

"What sort of name is that?"

"It's my Super Girl name."

"Your, what name?" asked Bailey, looking a little confused.

"It's my Super Girl name, and here's Solo, Angel and Momo," she continued, introducing the rest of the girls by the pseudonyms.

"Who and what are the Super Girls?" Bailey asked, trying to conceal her interest.

"Us," replied Roo.

"Then what are you?"

"Well… we were all like you, you know the new girl," said Momo.

"We didn't have friends either when we first arrived here."

"Who says I don't have any friends?" Bailey pouted.

There was an awkward silence in which Roo compressed her lips, Angel looked to the skies and Solo rolled her eyes, sighing.

"So we formed our own circle of friends," Angel continued enthusiastically, despite the spiky reception her enthusiasm was falling upon. "All you have to do to join us is befriend any girl who arrives at the school mid-term, and have your own Super Girl name of course!"

"How about 'Misery Guts'", said Solo under her breath, yet suspiciously loud enough to be heard, as was evidenced by Bailey's reaction.

"I heard that," she remonstrated.

"What a talent," replied Solo sarcastically.

"Solo!" exclaimed Roo, admonishing her by tone.

"Solo…?" remarked Bailey questioningly, "is that because no one wants to be around you?"

Solo parted her lips, presumably to retaliate, but Roo interjected, cutting her off before the fledgling argument took flight.

"Do you want to join us or not?" she asked, politely but firmly.

Bailey pondered for a moment.

"Alright then," she conceded.

"Good," Roo declared.

"Then you'll need a Super Girl name," she went on, looking sideways at Solo to ensure she didn't venture any more inflammatory suggestions. Solo raised her eyes snootily but remained silent.

"Let see," continued Roo, looking to Momo and Angel for inspiration.

"Do you have favourite things, colours or interests that might inspire a name?"

Bailey fell silent for a moment.

"I like cake," she declared.

"Anything else?" asked Angel, whilst Roo turned to wipe off her face, the grin she was finding difficult to conceal.

"You know those toffees that…?"

"How about we take the first two letters of your names?" interjected Momo, tactfully."

"How do you mean?" asked Bailey.

B for Bailey, B for Barnes, we could call you BB…what do you think?"

"Yes," agreed Roo, "it's short, sharp, I like it."

"Me too," agreed Angel.

"How about it 'BB'?" asked Momo, smiling warmly.

"Alright then," said Bailey, decidedly friendlier than she'd appeared up until that moment.

Then, there were seven.

CHAPTER 4

Miss Hoskins, Wrong?

Summer had come and gone with unforgivable haste. A new school year had begun, and the Super Girls found themselves back at the Stanley. Some weeks of the new term had passed and during break time the girls could be found occupying their usual spot in the school grounds. As Halloween neared they discussed excitedly their plans and costumes for the big night. Whilst the conversation went back and forth on one such occasion, Roo broke in, "trouble at three o' clock," she warned in hushed tones.

"Excuse me?" queried Willow.

Roo repeated herself, nodding as she spoke in the direction of said 'trouble'. Willow looked over BB's shoulder to see the plentiful figure of Miss Hoskins fast approaching. As she neared, the girls fanned out, whereupon they met with her steady gaze. Miss Hoskins drew to a sharp halt, scanning the group from left to right with a surly look fixed upon her face. Folding her arms under her large bosom she drew breath to speak, appearing to get considerably taller as she did so.

"So, which one of you was it?" she demanded in a cold, sinister tone of voice.

There was a brief silence lest she had not finished speaking, for anyone interrupting her would surely be banished to eternal damnation.

"Miss?" enquired Roo.

Miss Hoskins moved closer, her broad, wrinkled face not suffering scrutiny well at such close quarters.

"Don't *Miss*, me girl!" she thundered, her voice turning a little shrill, which was not a good sign.

"Which one of you let the fire extinguisher off in the gym?" she demanded.

"It wasn't one of us," implored Roo.

"Oh no of course, I was forgetting, you girls do everything together don't you?"

Willow opened her mouth to agree but before any words escaped her lips, Miss Hoskins spoke again.

"Two weeks' detention for the lot of you," she barked.

"Though if I had my way we'd still be caning girls too," she added, gleeful at the very thought of it. With that she turned and marched stiffly away.

"But Miss?" pleaded BB.

At the sound of BB's appeal, Miss Hoskins spun quickly and gracefully around in mid step, her face taut with rage, eyes narrowed and brow furrowed.

"Make it three weeks," she spat, angrily.

Then turning quickly again, she bustled away, assured she wouldn't be challenged a second time.

Roo and Solo shot BB a scornful glare; BB looked to the rest of the girls for support, shrugging her shoulders, uttering simply, "what…?"

Momo threw her arm around BB leading her away with the rest of the group.

"At least we'll all be together," said Momo enthusiastically, though by their silence the other girls did not share her sentiments.

The weekend before detention was due to begin evaporated quickly, as time tends to do when something unpleasant lay ahead. Monday morning and afternoon didn't account for much either, and as the latter petered out, the girl's detainment drew ever closer. They met as arranged outside the library, where their temporary but daily incarceration was to take place. At least six of them were there, unsurprisingly Momo had not yet arrived and Miss Hoskins was due any minute.

"How does that girl manage to be quite so late, so very often?" complained Willow. Miss Hoskins will be along any moment and if we're not all here when she arrives…"

Willow paused.

"Certain torture, followed by inevitable death," interjected Roo playfully.

"Oh do be serious Roo," protested Willow.

Moments passed, the rest of the girls became anxious, for still Momo was nowhere to be seen, or heard of for that matter.

Suddenly the sound of footsteps could be heard drawing near, heavy and even in nature.

Moments later the sound of much faster, lighter steps evidenced themselves.

"It's Momo!" cried Angel.

"Then the other steps must be Miss Hoskins," Wasp anxiously concluded.

As both sets of footsteps became louder and clearer, Miss Hoskins' to the left, Momo's to the right, it became impossible to tell who would arrive first. With anxious expressions all around, Roo decided it was time to act. After collecting up books from the other girls she threw them violently to the ground, the dull cracking sound they made resonated throughout the hallway.

"Whatever are you doing?" cried Willow, perplexed by Roo's actions.

"Willow you stay here," said Roo, "when you see Momo get

her to hurry up.

The rest of us will head Miss Hoskins off, we'll say we heard a great crash and were worried she'd had an accident of some sort.

Come on girls, let's go," and with an assured, little wink of her eye, Roo led the other girls swiftly away up the hall.

Rounding a corner, the group of five were confronted by Miss Hoskins marching towards them. They rushed noisily at her, adding credibility to their ruse. "Oh Miss, oh Miss," they chimed, creating as much distraction and delay as possible. For a moment Miss Hoskins looked startled and completely taken off guard, as she braced herself against their charge. These though were human traits, something she never displayed, or felt, apparently. One could have even been forgiven for thinking the menacing stare residing on her face, momentarily disappeared.

"Silence!" she bellowed, and immediately all was quiet.

"What is the meaning of this outrage?" she demanded.

The girls already silent, remained so, only Roo ventured to speak on their behalf.

"Oh Miss," she said as sincerely as she could.

"We heard such a terrible, loud noise and felt sure you may have had an accident of some sort, so we came to help."

Roo had never attended the school's drama club, but based on this performance it was evidently missing out. It was so good in fact that even Miss Hoskins seemed to pause for thought. Then as if disgusted with herself she snapped back to her usual cynical and suspicious demeanour, quickly denouncing the girls' concern.

Nonsense," she snarled, "you're up to something," her eyes narrowing at the thought of what it might be.

"Line up behind me," she barked, and as soon as the girls had, she marched them quickly towards the library.

Back there, Momo was running the last hundred yards or so of the hallway at Willow's frantic insistence. Pausing momentarily, Momo bent down, hurriedly removing her shoes so the noise of her footsteps didn't give her away to Miss Hoskins, who could be heard fast approaching. Moments later, breathless and rosy cheeked, she drew to a halt alongside a very relieved Willow.

"Upon my word Momo, could you not try to be on time at least once in your life?" she scorned her resignedly.

Momo gestured to catch her breath, then peering over Willow's shoulder her eyes widened at the sight of Miss Hoskins coming into view.

"Hush now Willow, Miss Hoskins is coming."

At this unwelcome news, Willow straightened her tie, flattened out her blazer and stood bolt upright. Coming to a halt in front of both her and Momo, Miss Hoskins surveyed the two girls, her piercing eyes seemingly almost able to read their thoughts.

"I see Miss Forbes Hamilton you do not share your cohorts concern for my wellbeing?" she scoffed.

"Oh yes Miss, I mean no Miss, well what I meant..."

"Enough child!" Miss Hoskins bellowed, before turning her attentions to Momo.

"So...you managed to be on time for once, did you girl?" she said, her words spoken slowly and purposefully.

"Yes Miss," replied Momo earnestly.

"Quite the healthy glow you have about you Miss Morrison?"

"Yes Miss."

"And what's this I see," she asked rhetorically, looking down at Momo's shoeless feet, "a bohemian detention perhaps?" she mocked.

"New shoes Miss, they were pinching my feet Miss."

"Is that so?" Miss Hoskins remarked; her tone and inflection conveying complete disbelief of Momo's account of events.

There was a silence as Miss Hoskins leaned uncomfortably close to Momo.

"I'll catch you later Miss Morrison," she said with a reassured, cold expression on her face.

"Right!" she barked, "everybody in now, run, run, run, don't keep me waiting."

The girls hurriedly filed into the library, breaking the pristine silence within, pulling chairs across the old, dark wooden floor and setting down their satchels and pencil cases. Once they were seated and silent, Miss Hoskins spoke again, her voice reverberating against the backdrop of quiet.

"Right, since we…" she paused, "or at least you girls are here on account of your misconduct, you will study female etiquette through the ages for the next three weeks. I will hand you over to Mrs. Hill now who will be reporting to me at the end of each evening. Though rest assured, I will be watching you too," she added menacingly. With that and a few words to Mrs. Hill, Miss Hoskins bustled out of the room.

"Do you think she'll really be watching us?" asked Wasp nervously once she could no longer hear 'bustling'.

"No," replied BB bluntly, "she's lying."

Wasp blushed a little and then fell back into chatting with the other girls. As the noise level escalated Mrs. Hill interjected.

"Quiet down ladies, remember you are in a library," she said firmly but kindly, not anything like the barbed orders and demands that ran rampant from Miss Hoskins' mouth. Mrs. Hill was a short broad sort of lady with dark, curly hair under which green eyes twinkled. The Stanley had been her employer for almost her entire life. She could seem quite strict, even rigid at times when flanked by her peers, but in the absence of them she was a good deal softer. She knew everything that was going on in the school, and if you ever confided in her, you could be sure that it would go with her to her grave.

"Miss?" enquired Wasp innocently.

"Yes dear," replied Mrs. Hill warmly.

"Does Miss Hoskins really see what's going on in the library even when she's not actually here?"

Mrs. Hill looked up from her work, peering over her horn-rimmed glasses.

"Why of course she does my dear," she replied with a smile and a little wink before returning to her work.

"You see," said BB, turning awkwardly in her chair to address Wasp.

"But Mrs. Hill said Miss Hoskins does watch us even when she's not here," countered Wasp.

"Yes," BB argued, "but then she smiled and winked,"

"I'm confused," conceded Wasp.

"You're not confused Wasp, your just plain gullible. If a person winks when they're saying something it means their pulling your leg."

Wasp sunk back in her chair; BB turned around, tutting and rolling her eyes as she so often did.

The two hours of detention passed surprisingly quickly with the liberal amount of chatting afforded by Mrs. Hill. Presently, footsteps could be heard echoing throughout the hallway, the hard, matronly footsteps of Miss Hoskins by the sounds of them. Mrs. Hill hushed the girls and made them ready to receive their jailer. Momentarily the large, wooden library door creaked loudly, as if pained at being opened with so little delicacy. Miss Hoskins filled the space it formerly occupied, her eyes surveying the room as soon as she entered it.

She marched stiffly over to Mrs. Hill's desk, her chest puffed out, her head held aloft and a sly look about her face.

"Well Mrs. Hill?" she rasped, "have they been any trouble?" Always half hoping there was some need for reprimand. Mrs. Hill looked over the rims of her glasses in a very considered way.

"Not at all Miss Hoskins," she reported brightly, "little angels every one of them."

"Hmm," muttered Miss Hoskins, her face stiff with disappointment.

"Angels!" she spat, for just the word itself was hard for her to say.

"Angels! why all seven of them on a good day wouldn't amount to one angel on a bad one. Thank you, Mrs. Hill," resumed Miss Hoskins grudgingly.

"Alright you girls may leave," she continued.

As the girls filed out, not a murmur escaping them, Miss Hoskins broke in.

"See you all tomorrow," she taunted with a sarcastic smile creeping across her face.

"Doesn't she have anything better to do, like polishing her gargoyles or something?" said Momo disdainfully, once out of ear shot. The rest of the girls laughed, though not too loud for fear of being overheard, and on that happy note they made their way to their respective homes.

On Wednesday, at four o'clock they began their third day of detention. Not quite an hour had passed when Miss Hoskins made a surprise appearance, bustling through the door in her usual bullish manner. Making her way quickly to Mrs. Hill's desk, she bent over to speak with her briefly before turning to face her audience. Though she had entered the room in her usual way, there was something different about Miss Hoskins on this occasion. Mrs. Hill arose from her chair, quietly tucking it under the desk before leaving the room. As she passed the girls, she gave them a little wink and a smile. Miss Hoskins made her way around the desk that had just been vacated. Spreading her arms wide, she leaned over it, peering at her captives.

"It would appear," she began, "it wasn't you girls who set off the fire extinguisher in the gym but other parties. As a result, your detention is to end immediately," she added with thinly veiled disappointment.

The girls all broke out in smiles, though they contained any thoughts of speaking for fear of Miss Hoskins changing her mind.

"On Friday," she resumed, "the fourth and fifth year pupils will be going on a trip to Horseforth Manor for Halloween. It is the Headmaster's wish you be allowed to join them, as you have been given detention due to someone else's wrong doing. Miss Worcester will provide you with all the necessary details when you see her for history class tomorrow, that will be all," she concluded. With that Miss Hoskins dismissed them and marched stiffly out of the library and down the corridor.

The girls quickly packed their things away, breaking into conversation as soon as she could no longer be heard.

"Didn't see that coming," said Roo.

"Indeed not," agreed Willow.

CHAPTER 5

A Witch's Proposition

In the morning the girls were all reunited in Miss Worcester's history class. After the lesson they were summoned to her desk. Miss Worcester was a tall, slender, bespectacled woman with suspiciously red hair. She was always perfectly groomed and always sported a scarf held together with a brooch of some sort. She was a woman of few words, most of them being delivered sharply and abruptly. On this particular occasion she didn't disappoint, gathering together the schedules for the girls' trip, silently and efficiently.

When finished, she looked up.

"You will all need one of these, Miss Forbes Hamilton please pass them along. Right, you girls are set, run along then," she added in a dismissive tone, waving her hand towards the door, gesturing for them to leave. As they filed out, Miss Worcester turned in her seat, putting on her glasses that otherwise hung about her chest on a thin, gold neck chain. Looking over them purposefully, she spoke again.

"Oh by the way you do know Horseforth Manor is haunted, don't you?"

Taking a few seconds to gauge the girls' reactions, she then casually returned to her work.

Once outside Wasp wasted no time in enquiring what Miss Worcester had meant.

"Is the house we are to visit, really haunted?" she asked in a worried tone.

"No of course it isn't," said BB "she was pulling your leg, like Mrs. Hill in the library the other day."

"But she didn't wink," Wasp remarked nervously.

"You will be perfectly safe with us Wasp," snapped Willow, after which she turned and abruptly left for her next lesson alone.

"What's wrong with her?" asked Angel, turning to Momo.

"I don't know, but she was pretty quiet on the way home last night too."

"Oh well, better get off to our next lesson, who could possibly want to miss Art Class?" replied Angel playfully.

After school the day before their impending visit, the girls agreed to stay over at Willow's house, as it had lots of rooms and was proximate to Horseforth Manor. They walked the mile or so there, talking excitedly about their sleepover and trip the following day.

Because Willow's mother and father were very wealthy people, the house in which they lived, was, as you might expect, very grand. Approaching the driveway, it stood before them, its central building flanked by the east and west wings. Its walls were greyish in colour, varying in shade and texture, etched on by decades of exposure to the weather.

Over the stone grew lush, green ivy, contrasting starkly to the sombre canvas onto which it clung. Tall, narrow leaded light windows stretched high up the three-storey facade. Pristine lawns, on which grew a stand of meticulously spaced trees completed the picture postcard vista.

They entered the grounds by means of a man-sized gate, that with its counterpart, flanked the two huge, arcaded gates at the centre.

Some of the other Super Girls had visited Willow's home on previous occasions, so were not surprised by the magnificence of it and splendour in which she lived.

Wasp however came from a large family of humble means and had not been to the house before.

"Is this where you live?" she asked, amazed at the sight before her.

Willow turned, "yes indeed," she said matter-of-factly, "at least when we're not living in France of course."

"What's in France?" asked BB quizzically.

"The French I imagine," Roo quipped, at which the other girls laughed, except BB who pulled a face.

"Oh," said Willow, returning to her conversation with Wasp, "our other house."

"Oh of course, silly me," said BB playfully.

"I can't go in there," said Wasp. "I wouldn't know how to act or anything."

Willow put her hand on Wasp's shoulder and looked at her squarely.

"It is I Wasp who does not know how to act."

"I'm sorry?" said Wasp appearing confused.

"This morning, I snapped at you, forgive me."

"Oh, I'd forgotten."

"Thank you," said Willow earnestly, "now come along up to the house, no need to be anything but yourself."

The girls resumed their trek, arriving after a couple of minutes at a dark, wooden door. Beside it, hung a large crudely fashioned, black, metal chain, attached to the wall by means of a similarly fashioned angle iron. Willow pulled on the chain and inside the house the sound of muted bells could be heard clanging away at its command.

"Why don't you just walk in through the door Willow?" asked Roo.

"Well, its Geoffrey our butler, he likes to open the door for me, he insists a lady should never have to open them for herself."

A few moments passed before he appeared.

"Ah! Good afternoon Miss Portia," he said in his usual dignified manner.

"I see that you have brought us some company," he continued, smiling as he spoke.

"Yes Geoffrey, these are my friends, could you please show them to the kitchen whilst I go and say hello to mummy and daddy."

"Of course, Miss Portia."

Geoffrey ushered the girls in, whilst 'Miss Portia' went off to locate her parents. Once again Wasp was amazed, for inside the house was more like a museum than were someone lived.

The floor of the reception area was covered in black and white geometrically placed, marble tiles. Rising from them, dark, carved, wooden panels handed off to thick, red and gold flocked wallpaper. Great paintings in gilded frames peppered the vast space. The ceiling too, was decorated with a huge fox hunting scene set against the backdrop of the English countryside.

"Come now ladies, let me show you into the kitchen," said Geoffrey.

"I'm sure we can find you something nice to eat and drink," he continued, beckoning the way with his pristine, white, gloved hand. Some minutes later, Willow rejoined the rest of the girls, flushed from running down stairs and through the vast expanse of the great house she called home.

The afternoon quickly conceded to the evening, by which time the light outside was fading. A large, ornate, wooden grandfather clock in the main hall chimed defiantly on the hour, the sound of which carried throughout the lower part of the house. After its point was conveyed, it resumed more modest behaviour, ticking gently. The girls had agreed to retire to Willow's room to play a board game of some sort before bed. As they tramped up the large, winding staircase to the third floor, the old wooden boards heaved and groaned beneath their collective weight. At the top, inside Willow's room, Geoffrey had set up a make shift dormitory so that none of the girls would be apart from each other.

"So what shall we play?" asked Solo, looking in a large cupboard where every board game that ever was, resided.

Momo went over to join her, reaching in to make a selection. "How about this one?" she suggested, showing it to Solo.

Solo nodded in approval.

"Everyone ok with haunted house?" Momo asked the rest of the girls, and after three more yeses, the decision was carried. BB and Wasp were otherwise engaged trying to bounce each other off the giant, four poster bed. Momo and Solo set up the pieces and shuffled the cards, whilst the rest of the girls positioned themselves in a semi-circle around the board. Once the order of play was decided the game began with Angel being the first to throw. A large, bright, imposing moon hung in a clear, dark blue sky outside, its glow inviting itself into Willow's room through the old leaded light windows. After nearly an hour or so, only Momo, Solo and Willow remained in the game. Willow picked up the dice to take her next turn. Shaking it in the cup she threw it out onto the board where it resolved on six. Picking up the witch figure she moved it the requisite number of spaces, counting them off as she went. Landing on a cryptic clue, Willow took the corresponding card and held it before her. There was a brief silence as her eyes darted from left to right reading the lines upon it.

"What does it say? what does it say?" enquired BB impatiently, moving behind Willow so she could read it herself. Willow remained silent, her face turning so pale she had become almost transparent; to stop her hands trembling she held the card close to her chest.

"Whatever can be the matter Willow?" exclaimed Solo, making her way over to her. Snapping back to reality, for it seemed the poor girl was in a trance, she simply said, "it's getting late, perhaps we should finish off in the morning." With that she excused herself and left, trying in vain to conceal her haste.

The other girls sat stunned, except Wasp who lay asleep and had been for some time.

"Hand me the clue card please BB," said Solo. BB complied, and with the rest of the girls closely gathered around, she began to read it.

"A gap in time,
A secret doorway,
Seven pieces to win,
Any less and you will pay."

"What about this clue could have upset Willow so?" mused Solo.

"Read it again," urged Momo.

"That card isn't in this game," she concluded, once Solo had finished.

"What do you mean?" asked Solo with a quizzical expression.

"That clue, the one you read, it doesn't belong to this game."

"How do you know?"

"I have it at home, I used to play it with Angel when we were the only two Super Girls."

"Is this true Angel?"

"Momo's right, we've played this game a hundred times since we first met, and this clue isn't part of it."

"Maybe it's a new version," suggested BB.

"No," said Angel emphatically, it's the same one alright, but a good suggestion BB all the same."

The riddle caused Solo to contort her face.

"Read it one more time," insisted Angel, "but very slowly."

Silence prevailed whilst Solo carefully picked her way through the verse, looking for some clue hidden in the text.

As soon as the last word fell from her lips however, a brilliant bolt of lightning bleached the room and a clap of thunder rattled mercilessly throughout the house.

Everyone dived onto the bed, quickly pulling the thick, velvet curtains behind them. Wasp woke up, startled by the sudden commotion.

"It's ok" said Solo, assuring those evidently more startled than she, "it's just thunder and lightning." Drawing one of the curtains back, she made her way over to the window to check.

"I'll come with you," said Momo, who promptly followed.

Upon reaching it, the two of them looked out at the beautiful autumn night, unfettered by clouds and bathed in the moon's glow.

One by one heads popped from behind the curtains that enveloped the bed. "Everything alright?" enquired BB sheepishly.

"Yes BB," Solo assured her, a little grin passing across her face. She turned to Momo, her expression quite altered.

"But it's not all right is it Momo?" she said, her complexion growing pale.

"I ask you? thunder and lightning on a night such as this and Willow just upping and leaving like that. Something's wrong, what do you think?" she continued, her tone, grave.

"I do too, but I cannot imagine what?" Momo replied similarly.

"I'm going to look for Willow, perhaps you can distract the others.

We don't all want to be milling about the house at such a late hour, do we?"

"Ok, but be careful," cautioned Solo. When an opportunity presented itself,

Momo slipped quietly out of the room unnoticed.

Creeping down the hallway careful not to be seen or heard, she made her way to the top of the landing. Small, evenly spaced sconce lights partially illuminated the stairwell. Momo sat at its threshold, tucking her knees in and wrapping her arms around them, listening for any voices coming from below. She could hear nothing, so raising herself up she slowly and cautiously continued on. Standing on the first break in the stairwell, where they doubled back down to the next floor, she paused again. Satisfied there was nothing out of the ordinary to report she began descending the next flight of stairs. Then suddenly, *clangggg!* the grandfather clock chimed the passing of the last hour. Though it might well have been chiming the last minute of Momo's life, startling her so, she could barely catch her breath. Gathering herself, though it wasn't easy, she resumed her passage downwards. Standing in the hallway of the second floor, Momo decided for some reason, she knew not why, Willow would be found in the lower level of the house.

Descending the last flight of stairs, she crept gingerly into the kitchen, but Willow wasn't there, nor was any other soul. Switching off the light she backed steadily out of the doorway and headed into the library, but once again she was to be disappointed. Making her way further into the heart of the house she came upon a door slightly ajar, from which a shaft of light intruded into the dark passage way. Sensing Willow was in the great gallery, Momo slowly and carefully peeked through the aperture. Scanning the room as best she could with such limited scope, Momo caught sight of her, luckily though, she was facing away. Standing before one of the great paintings, Willow was motionless, transfixed on the image within the frame. Momo had been to the house on a couple of occasions and recognised the painting as that of Willow's Great-great uncle, Colonel Montgomery Forbes Hamilton. Willow continued to study the portrait, Momo continued her vigil. Then without warning or sign, Willow spun around, as if she'd suddenly become aware of being watched. Momo wasted no time, rushing back through the house as quickly and quietly as possible. It was evident by the sound of Willow's footsteps however, that she was determined to find out who her company had been. Losing ground to her long, lean pursuer, Momo arrived at the bottom of the stairs, leaping over Percival who had taken up residence to sleep there the night. Waking with an indignant frown on his face, he rose to his feet creating a perfect barrier for Willow to surmount. Lucky he did, for she'd been gaining on Momo fast. Arriving on the third floor, Momo lifted her pace, dashing across the hallway towards Willow's bedroom.

Slowing, only to gently open and close the door behind her, she dived onto one of the makeshift beds in which Solo lay. Fully clothed and breathless she hid under the blankets and pretended to be asleep, half expecting Willow to enter the room at any moment.

"What on earth are you doing?" asked Solo in a raised hushed tone, looking every bit as indignant as Percival had. "Shhh, I'll tell you in the morning," said Momo cryptically.

CHAPTER 6

Willow's Secret

The next morning the girls assembled in the main kitchen where the servants prepared all the meals and ate theirs. They sat at a long, dark, wooden plank table on heavy, old, matching leather chairs. There was more than enough room, for the table seated twenty people at full capacity. Willow, the host, arrived second from last. Avoiding publicly scorning her for not being the first, the look on her father's face displayed better anything he could otherwise convey. Momo was, as usual, marvellously late but perhaps if she hadn't been, there would have been concerns as to her health. When she did eventually arrive, she found the rest of the girls chatting excitedly about their impending trip, except Willow, who was somewhat removed from the anticipation.

After breakfast, everyone gathered up their things and made for the entrance gates to the house, where it had been arranged the school bus pick them up. Solo cunningly devised it so she could sit next to Momo, many seats removed from Willow. Once the bus had pulled away, its engine whirring noisily as it tried to pick up momentum, Solo began her line of enquiry.

"So, did you catch up with Willow last night?" she asked in a whisper, anxious to hear Momo's reply.

"Yes I did," Momo answered with a puzzled expression.

"And?" asked Solo, her eyes widening in anticipation of some news.

"Well," it was very odd, as I found her in the great gallery looking at one of the paintings... well more like staring at it really."

There was a brief pause before Solo spoke again.

"Which one?"

"It was the one of her great, great uncle, Colonel Montgomery Forbes Hamilton."

Solo fell quiet, seemingly because a thought or an idea was forming in her head.

"How was she looking at it?" she resumed.

"Well, as if transfixed, as if," Momo paused, "as if she wished she were able to talk to him."

The girls fell quiet, the roar of the old, diesel engine heaving its burden up the steep incline towards Horseforth Manor filled the silence. Some minutes later the old house came into view, the imposing spectacle augmented by the early morning mist which hung around it.

Although Willow's house was extremely large and just as spectacular on the outside, Horseforth was singular, in that it had a definite presence to it. Whilst you gazed upon it, unlike most buildings, it seemed to gaze back at you. Continuing towards the entrance gates, the bus drew to a halt, its brakes squealing lazily. To the right of it lay the gatehouse, a little building fashioned from the same stone as Horseforth itself. A short-wizened man with almost white hair appeared from within. From the pocket of his dark blue three-piece suit he pulled a gold watch attached to a chain. He greeted the driver whilst peering at it through his small round rimmed spectacles.

"Running a little late, aren't you?" he remarked as if requiring some explanation.

The driver leant out of the bus window.

"The fog," he said apologetically, pointing at it.

"Alright," conceded the gatekeeper, "on you go."

The bus pulled slowly through the main gates, the gatekeeper waving at its occupants with a kindly smile as they passed him. About halfway down the drive however, the bus began to falter, coughing and spluttering, finally coming to an undignified halt. The driver tried to restart the bus but to no avail, the bus had made its decision. Climbing down from his seat to take a look under the bonnet, his attention was stolen by the gatekeeper, rushing up to join him. When he drew closer it was apparent by his expression all was not well.

"Got some trouble there Mr.?" he panted.

"She seems to have conked out," said the driver scratching his head with a bemused expression. Moving around to the front of the bus he lifted the bonnet to check underneath.

"You won't find the answer under there Sir," said the gatekeeper with an air of certainty.

Turning his head whilst looking over the bus's engine, the driver enquired as to what the gatekeeper was speaking of.

"Why, the curse of course Sir,"

Satisfied there was no apparent problem, the driver slammed the bonnet down hard and made his way around to the side of the bus. Trying to conceal a smile, he broke out.

"You don't believe in that old wives' tale, do you?"

"Oh I do Sir," said the gatekeeper, with a stony expression.

"This town has been under the curse long before I was born, and will be long after I'm gone."

"Well," said the driver, seeing that he didn't share the gate keeper's opinion.

"Let's give her another try, shall we?"

Jumping back into the bus, he reclaimed his seat and turned the keys in the ignition. The engine turned over and over and over some more, but still didn't fire up. The driver, whose face was a little flushed, turned to the gatekeeper standing just outside the doors.

"Probably just needs another turn," he said with a nervous chuckle. The gatekeeper remained silent, shaking his head in a solemn manner. Again, the driver turned the engine, but again the result was the same, nothing.

Seeing the bus wasn't going to move, he turned to his passengers.

"Ok everybody, time for a little walk," he announced.

The bus resounded with the moans and groans of the disgruntled group of children, as they grudgingly rose to their feet to file out. The driver got off last and turned to the gatekeeper.

"Do you have a telephone I can use to call the breakdown lorry, please?" he enquired.

"I do Sir, but you won't need it."

"Why ever not?" said the driver with a quizzical expression.

"The bus will go just fine if you put her in reverse, she doesn't want to go any nearer to the house, that's all Sir."

"Because of the curse?" said the driver flippantly.

"Yes that's right Sir, you'll see presently," said the gatekeeper, narrowing his eyes.

The drive reluctantly hauled himself back into his seat, then with a wry smile put the bus into reverse and turned the engine over. To his amazement it leapt back to life, firing up as soon as the key was turned, its engine purring like a race car. His face fell into an expression of disbelief before a more frightened look beset it. With thumbs up and a little grin, the gatekeeper waved him back down the driveway. Once on the main road, he sped away, leaving a cloud of smoke as testament to his haste. Meanwhile Miss Worcester had marched her unlikely foot soldiers to the Manor's main entrance. There they awaited the arrival of Mr. Beckinsale, the establishment's curator and historian. A few moments passed before he appeared, issuing from the house as if propelled by a spring. His thin, wiry frame bounded down the stairs with all the enthusiasm of a person who had just received their first group of visitors ever. Stopping in front of them, he bid everybody good morning, wringing his hands whilst he spoke.

After he had finished his introduction, he gestured for everyone to follow him.

"Let us now go and expose the mysteries of Horseforth Manor," he said, as if he were a magician about to reveal the final and most spectacular illusion of his act.

The rest of the morning he led the group from one room to the next, all of them resplendent, immaculately kept, and brimming with stories and tales. Before breaking for lunch, the group's tour concluded in the great ballroom, inside of which, huge chandeliers hung perfectly aligned from a beautifully decorated ceiling that seemed to stretch to the heavens. Great gilded mirrors punctuated and filled the spaces between the round topped windows, adorned with thick, lush, blood red velvet curtains.

At the far end of the great ballroom Mr. Beckinsale had chairs arranged in a semi-circle, for he had a very particular tale to tell about this part of the house. After everyone was seated, he wasted no time launching into a story which he'd doubtless told on hundreds of occasions. All eyes were fixed forwards, although out of the corner of one of hers, Momo noticed Willow's were not. They were cast down, with her left hand positioned to obscure them. Momo dug Solo in the ribs for she was the most proximate, at which Solo turned towards her with a scowl on her face.

"What do you want?" she asked with all the indignation a hushed tone could possibly convey.

Momo nodded to where Willow was sitting.

"Look!" she said, "what do you make of that?"

Solo's expression changed, turning quizzical.

As she was about to speak, Mr. Beckinsale broke in.

"Ladies, please, if I could have your attention," he said meekly.

"Oh yes Sir, sorry Sir," the two girls chorused.

"Quite alright," he said, quickly returning to his story. Moments later, the dull scraping sound of a chair being moved across the wooden floor broke Mr. Beckinsale's concentration a second time.

Willow stood up, hurriedly excusing herself as she began threading her way between the chairs, quickly making her exit.

Mr. Beckinsale, looking somewhat confused, broke in again.

"Is there something wrong Miss?" he enquired awkwardly, raising his hand as if somehow that would help.

But Willow was gone before the last words left his mouth. Thinking quickly Momo jumped up from her seat, "no breakfast Sir, I think she's feeling a little sick."

"Perhaps you should go and help her Miss…?" Mr. Beckinsale paused helplessly.

"Morrison, Sir." said Momo, quickly relieving him of his awkwardness.

"Yes indeed Miss Morrison," he said, adding "thank you."

Momo thanked Mr. Beckinsale in return and hurriedly retraced Willow's footsteps, disappearing out of the great ballroom as she had only seconds before.

Some moments later she found Willow outside in the grounds of the estate. Perched on a low, white stone wall, she sat motionless, her head bowed. Momo remained distant for a minute or two, doing nothing more than keeping a vigil on her stricken friend as she had done the previous night. Presently she approached.

"Willow, whatever can be wrong?" she asked. Willow lifted her head, her eyes were watery as if she was saddened to the point of tears.

"Darling Momo," she said taking her hands in hers.

"I have a secret that I have kept from all of you."

"We all have secrets," said Momo in an effort to comfort her.

"Not like this one Momo, I feel sure, not like this one."

"Why don't you try me?" suggested Momo, kindly.

There was a brief pause as Willow gathered herself.

"Very well, you would be hearing the story right now had you stayed in the great ballroom, anyway."

At this, Momo's curiosity was engaged and she waited with great eagerness for Willow's explanation of her recent strange behaviour.

Willow took a deep breath, flattened out her blazer with the palms of her hands and straightened the knot in her tie, as if presenting before a large assembly.

"Momo, do you know who owns this house?"

"No" replied Momo, her face pinched with curiosity.

"This house belongs to the Forbes Hamilton family."

"Your family?" said Momo, shocked by the revelation.

"Yes Momo, it belongs to our family, not that we ever intend to use it again, that's why it is in the hands of the trustees as a museum. You see Momo, this house has a story attached to it," Willow paused, "well, not just a story, more of a legend really."

"A legend?" repeated Momo excitedly, "do tell."

"Very well," agreed Willow.

"Over a hundred years ago my Great-great uncle, Colonel Montgomery Forbes Hamilton, 'Mongo' to his friends, lived in this very home," Willow began, nodding in the direction of the house.

"For many years he was without a wife and seemingly had no one in mind.

Eventually it came to light that his heart belonged to one woman and one woman alone, her name was Emily Louise Russell.

Though her name mattered not, what was of great consequence however, was the fact that she was a commoner; indeed, she was a lady in service of this very house. Added to this it had long been suspected she was a witch."

"A witch?!" exclaimed Momo.

"Yes," said Willow, "but a white witch. Anyhow, on return from one of his trips to India, for he was there during the British occupation, he vowed he would marry Emily Louise, regardless of her lack of status. When he did come back, he bought a gift for her as a symbol of his intentions."

"What sort of gift?" asked Momo, her eyes fixed upon Willow.

"It was an urn," continued Willow "though not just any old urn, this was The Urn of Sabu."

"The urn of what?" queried Momo.

"The Urn of Sabu," repeated Willow.

"The Urn of Sabu was a coveted Indian artefact, used only in the marriage ceremonies of Royals and those who were very, very important in society. It was believed to possess magical powers.

Before leaving India, it was gifted to my Great-great uncle as a symbol of the people's esteem and affection for him. You see he was a very kind, compassionate man and although the country was under British occupation, he always insisted his men be just and fair."

"What happened next?" asked Momo impatiently.

"Well," continued Willow, "this is where things take a turn for the worst. My Great-great uncle had but one vice and that was, he was a gambler. Consequently, he had run up huge debts, and because they were so large he had no way of paying them off.

The only solution was for him to quit Horseforth and move

into more modest accommodation, lease Horseforth out and borrow against it."

"Sounds like a good plan," said Momo.

It was, except for one obstacle, that obstacle was his father, Roland Forbes Hamilton.

Roland did not hold this particular son in very high esteem, insisting he was a waster."

Roland however, still owned Horseforth and in order for my Great-great uncle Montgomery to put the debt repayment plan into action, he needed his approval.

Roland agreed, but made one stipulation; under no circumstances was my Great-great uncle to marry Emily Louise.

If he disobeyed him he would be disowned and cut out of the family's estate forever."

"And?" said Momo, eyes wide open, anxious to hear more.

"Well," resumed Willow, "my Great-great uncle stood firm, knowing if he was disowned, his creditors would be paid by his father to avoid disgracing the family's good name and reputation.

He would still have Emily, which was enough for him, as he truly loved her.

One night, after my uncle had told Roland of his intentions, he went to Emily with the urn to propose marriage.

At last he thought, as he made his way to the great ballroom, they would be together. His intention was to tell her of events, propose, and then dance one last waltz in the great ball room before he was thrown out of the house forever.

On hearing the news however, Emily flew in to a violent rage, the likes of which my Great-great uncle had never before seen.

Indeed, she was so incensed, she took the sacred urn and threw it, sending it crashing to the floor and shattering into pieces, seven to be exact.

THE SUPER GIRL SEVEN

It seemed Emily was only ever interested in my Great-great uncle's money, and when she knew she could not have it, she lost control.

Here's where the legend takes over."

"Yes, yes," said Momo leaning closer into Willow.

"Legend has it that if the urn was ever deliberately broken, it would unleash terrible evil. Emily assumed this evil and went over to the dark side."

Momo put her hand over her open mouth, "oh my!" she exclaimed.

"Wait," insisted Willow "there's more."

"There is?" Momo replied, her face all astonishment.

"Oh yes, lots more. After this incident my Great-great uncle disappeared and was never ever seen again. Rumour has it, Emily actually killed him. No evidence was ever found, though it is believed by some, she paid to have his body dumped over the side of a freight ship one night. Others believe that prior to his murder she turned him into a monkey."

"Why ever would she do such a thing?"

"Well, when my great-great uncle was in India, he would write to Emily.

In his letters, he would complain about the heat and the monkeys indigenous to the region.

They would steal food, leave droppings everywhere and

generally make a nuisance of themselves. Knowing this, it was Emily's wicked plan he died as one of them.

To ensure enduring misery, she created *The Labyrinth* for the monkey's spirit to wander in for evermore.

Just for sport, she hid the seven pieces of the urn inside, giving minuscule hope of liberation from its torment.

Myth has it that if the urn is put back together, the labyrinth will collapse, freeing anything trapped within it."

"Your Great-great uncle?"

"Well at least his spirit."

"Is that it?" Momo asked, as if needing to rest a little, if it weren't.

"Not quite," said Willow, who was in full stride of her story.

Momo took a breath as if to prepare herself, "ok, go on," she urged her.

"Some time later, Emily attached herself to a doctor.

Though he did not have the position in society my Great-great uncle enjoyed, he was not at all badly off for money. He however, wanted children, the idea of which Emily loathed, but she produced one to keep him happy.

She never loved the child, in fact she hated it, bitterly resenting it until the day she died. That child grew up as you may expect, hating children, though she produced one too, ironically a girl; Sarah Jane Hoskins...*Miss Hoskins!*"

Momo's head shot around, "where, where?" she panted.

Willow smiled, "no Momo, the girl child I speak of is, *Miss Hoskins.*"

Momo's face drained of its colour.

"You mean Miss Hoskins... our Miss Hoskins... *The Dragon Lady?!*"

"The very same."

Falling quiet, Momo wrestled with the pieces of Willow's story.

"Emily did die then?" she asked after some moments in silence.

"Well yes, though some say witches do not die, they just enter other realms, in Emily's case, the labyrinth. Before she left this world however, it is said and believed by most that she put a curse on the town."

"On West Denton?" Momo asked.

"No, on Sutton Althorpe."

"Why on Sutton?"

"She was brought up in the workhouses there without proper food or shelter.

She longed to be free of her bonds and rich like those who lived in West Denton.

So she cursed the town which had caused her so much pain and suffering, along with those she wanted so badly to escape from, the poor."

Silence prevailed between the two friends, Momo looked at Willow squarely.

"What do you believe Willow, the myth or the facts?"

Willow paused to consider her answer.

"Well," she began, "mostly I've believed in the facts, but there have been occurrences over the years that I cannot rationally explain."

"Can I ask what?"

Before Willow had time to answer, she was interrupted by voices emanating from behind the doors close to the low wall, where she and Momo were sitting. Shortly after, the rest of the Super Girls appeared. On spotting Momo and Willow they hastened to join them. BB came into sharp focus first, eyes glistening, face flushed from running.

"So are you one too?" she blurted out.

"One what?" replied Willow through pursed lips.

"A witch of course, silly."

Solo arrived in time to catch BB's less than subtle enquiry.

"Hush you silly girl, what sort of question is that to ask someone?"

"Well I was just wondering."

"Then don't," said Solo scornfully.

BB pulled her usual face, but said nothing in her defence.

The other three girls arrived, assembling around Willow and Momo too.

"So is it all true?" asked Roo.

Willow's sullen expression met Roo's gaze.

"Depends what you've heard," she replied coyly.

"Well you know, you're Great-great uncle, Emily Louise, the labyrinth and all the rest of it."

"Yes," said Willow exhaling audibly, as if she'd had this very conversation one too many times.

"It's all true."

"Why so glum Willow?" asked Angel cheerfully.

"Well I cannot imagine any of you wanting anything to do with me now, after all, I am a witch."

Willow ended her sentence by shooting BB a scornful glare, at which BB averted her eyes.

"Why not?" said Angel, puzzled that Willow could think such a thing.

"Well let's just say when most people hear the story they assume I am a witch too, and the misfortunes of Sutton Althorpe rest upon me and my family."

"I think it's great," said Angel with a big grin.

Willow looked at the rest of the girls searchingly to see what they thought. To her complete surprise, they too, were both excited by the story and anxious to know more.

"This," said Solo "is why you ended up at the Stanley with the rest of us, isn't it?"

Willow's expression changed to one of surprise.

"How do you know that Solo?"

"Some weeks before you joined us, I went over to the West Denton library to research something for our school project.

Anyway, whilst I was there I happened upon an article in the West Denton Chronicle about your family's history and the curse on Sutton Althorpe.

It wasn't a very fair piece of journalism as I remember; I think the writer just wanted to stir people up. When after a few weeks you came to the Stanley, I felt sure you had been driven out of your previous school by the rumours the article generated.

"You mean you knew the whole time Solo?" questioned Willow.

"Yes, we all knew."

"Then you have discussed me behind my back?" Willow continued, her expression stiffening.

"This is a school Willow, not a convent. We all knew from one source or another, but we chose not to discuss it, at least not at length. We made a collective decision to ignore the gossip and rumours and get to know you for ourselves."

"Did it not bother you what people thought of me and my family?" asked Willow, searching the faces of the six girls.

"I think I speak for all us misfits," said Solo with a smile

"Speak for yourself," protested BB.

"Especially BB," Solo continued, her smile broadening.

"We are the Super Girls, and the Super Girls stick together."

"So," Angel interjected.

"What happened last night during the game of haunted house, do you think that had something to do with all of this curse business?"

"Well," replied Willow, her eyes narrowing in thought. "It was quite strange do you not think?"

"But that clue card could have come from another game and got mixed up with the one we were playing," said Wasp.

"As for the thunder and lightning, well it was probably just an electrical storm that passed over very quickly," she continued, nervously trying to explain away the previous night's events.

"By show of hands then, who amongst us thinks there is something odd going on?" asked willow.

Solo, Momo, Angel, and Roo, put their hands in the air without hesitation; Wasp's remained firmly in her pockets, belying perhaps, what she truly thought.

"BB what say you?" asked Willow.

"I don't believe in ghosts and witches, I think it's all nonsense," she replied dismissively.

"But you have more to tell, do you not?" asked Momo.

"Yes indeed I do," said Willow ominously.

"Just before you all joined us I was about to tell Momo something that you would not have heard from Mr. Beckinsale.

"Gather round," she said, resuming her story.

"Some years ago, whilst we summered at our other house in France, a famous circus came to town. I cannot remember the name, as I was only about six or seven years old at the time. Anyway, I wanted to go, of course. Not just because it was the biggest and best travelling circus in the country but because it was also accompanied by the fair.

For weeks before, I worried my mother at every opportunity I got to take me, and eventually she agreed.

My mother you see didn't really agree with fairs and the like, she felt they were where the 'common people' gathered.

Strangely though when we got there she became completely altered, as if this whole other world had been going on about her and she'd been missing out on it. Before we left that day she decided, whilst riding the wave of mixing with the common folk, we would have our palms read. Usually she never held with such practices, denouncing them as a load of old 'mumbo jumbo', but on this day she was oddly suggestible.

So off we went into this colourful, old caravan where an old gypsy woman resided.

My mother went first and after she was finished, she encouraged me to have my palm read, which I can remember feeling quite uncomfortable about.

However, seeing that she had taken me to the fair, I thought perhaps I should comply with her wishes."

"Then what happened?" begged a wide-eyed BB.

"I thought you didn't believe in witches and ghosts BB," Solo remarked pointedly.

"Well I don't," BB snapped, her cheeks flushing. "I just thought it was an interesting story, that's all."

"Do go on Willow," Solo urged.

"Well, where was I? oh yes, the gypsy woman," Willow resumed.

"She summoned me over to her table. I remember it being covered with a faded, white, lace cloth, on top of which an old, oil lamp burned, giving off a very distinctive smell. She sat across from me, her gaunt wrinkled face softened by the meagre light cast upon it. About her head, I recall she wore a scarf, emblazoned with a floral pattern in reds, yellows, oranges and black, hanging from which were little thin gold coins that jangled when she moved.

Turning, slowly sideways, she asked me to bring my chair closer. My arms were only small, and I could not reach over the table as my mother had.

Gesturing me to sit, she took one of my hands in hers, briefly looking at my palm before turning her gaze towards me. I remember being mesmerised, not afraid, but transfixed, studying the eyes that had studied so many before mine. It was as if they were the sum of all the joy and pain she had seen and predicted.

Returning to the examination of my palm, she ran her thin, wizen fingers from one point to another. After some moments her expression turned distinctly serious.

Madame, she said addressing my mother, you must pull up a chair and witness this reading at close quarters. My mother, quite perplexed, did as she was asked, after which the gypsy woman resumed her work. Madame, she repeated her tone cold and forbidding.

Your daughter has been born into a troubled legacy. You have, by giving her life, foisted great responsibility upon her shoulders. My mother's face drained, though I knew not why. I have the initials of a man's name upon my lips, nod only if you recognise them, but do not speak, insisted the gypsy woman. M F H, she uttered weakly. At the sound of this my mother became fidgety, seemingly undecided as to what to do with her hands to keep them still.

He does not rest as he should, continued the gypsy woman, he cannot, he will not. Suddenly, she stiffened and was thrown back in her chair as if she had been hit by lightning. Still, she kept a desperate grip on my hand.

Slowly it weakened and with failing voice she uttered, seven, *only when there are seven*. Then she slumped lower in her rickety old chair, exhausted. Mother threw more than enough money to cover both readings on the table, grabbed my hand, and pulled me towards the door. Without warning the old gypsy woman awoke from her daze, her eyes popping open as if on springs.

My mother yelped, feeling the clairvoyant's grip upon her wrist, reeling us both in towards her.

Strengthening her grip, she drew us closer. You must take care of your child Madame, she warned, for she is one of the chosen.

With that, the eyes that had been so piercing, started to flicker like an old bulb about to expire. Her grip faltering, she rasped weakly, *when there are seven, when there are seven*. Finally, she slumped back again, her arm dropping limply to one side of the chair. Come darling, I remember my mother saying, let us go whilst we have the chance, and with that we hurried away."

Willow paused to break from her story.

"What happened next?" asked BB impatiently.

"Nothing, that is it, it was never spoken of again, and I had forgotten all about it until last night."

"This secret doorway, what does it mean?" asked Roo.

"I have no idea," replied Willow shaking her head.

"Could there be a secret doorway in this house that you don't know of?"

"I don't think so, I know every door on every floor, and what is on the other side of it," Willow replied with absolute certainty.

"How about that one between the first and second floor at the turn of the stairs near the entrance hall?" asked Wasp.

"That one felt decidedly creepy, when I passed by it this morning."

Willow fell quiet, a puzzled look beset her.

"Darling Wasp," she said, "there isn't a door between the first and second floor in that part of the house, that's one of the turrets. If you put a door there, people would open it and go tumbling half a floor down onto the ground outside. You must be mistaken," she concluded emphatically.

"No I am not," said Wasp, more assertively than any of the girls had ever known her to be.

A few moments passed.

"Let's go!" said Roo, and the girls all sped off at once, none of them in any doubt where they were heading, or why.

As they sprinted into the building as if chasing for the finishing line of the one hundred yard dash on sports day, Mr. Beckinsale appeared before them.

"Ah! just the girls I was looking for," he said brightly.

"Time for this afternoon's session," he continued pointing at his watch purposefully.

The girls' faces fell in unison, indeed, so obvious was it that Mr. Beckinsale was prompted to comment.

"Do you not like my lectures? am I perhaps not able to relate to young people as I thought I could?" he said with a disillusioned expression on his face.

"Oh no Sir," said Roo as she most confidently took up Mr. Beckinsale's arm, marching him back from whence he came.

"Not at all Sir, it's just we've been tending to our friend who had to leave the ballroom early and have missed our lunch because of it. We were hoping to get something quickly, from the cafeteria." said Roo, to account for the girl's collective disappointment at the sight of him.

Mr. Beckinsale considered their plight for a moment, and then his face lit up as if he had just discovered the wheel.

"Let me escort you to the kitchen," he said exuberantly, "I'll inform cook of your situation and see if she can rustle you up something.

I'll hold the afternoon session off for fifteen to twenty minutes, so you'll have time to eat."

"Oh thank you Sir," said Roo looking up at Mr. Beckinsale with a little twinkle in her eye, enough to make the poor man blush.

Presently, he led the girls down into the basement of the house where the main kitchen was situated. Their voices resonated as they threaded their way through the cold, poorly lit corridors underneath the great building's main floor. As the party drew nearer the kitchen, they heard the dull clanking sound of pots and pans filtering out into the otherwise desolate passage way. Arriving there, they found three women bustling around the steamy cavern. Mr. Beckinsale gave a little cough as a discreet signal of his presence, one which was lost above the hubbub of a kitchen running at full speed.

"I say," said Mr. Beckinsale, raising a hand in the air meekly to attract attention. One of the ladies, a short broad woman who wore her silver-grey hair in a tight bun, turned around.

"Can I 'elp you Sir," she asked in a brusque, almost Dickensian, cockney accent.

"Oh yes," said Mr. Beckinsale, somewhat surprised the lady had bothered to answer him at all.

"Mrs. Hatchet?" he said clasping his hands together, before pausing.

"Ruby," he continued, at which the lady's steely grey eyes brightened, her harsh expression giving way to a smile.

"Yes deary," she said, as if she were Mr. Beckinsale's aunt or grandmother.

"I wonder if you might feed these young ladies, they have been indisposed in the care of their friend and have completely missed their lunch."

"Well of course I will Mr. Beckinsale Sir," she replied, ushering the girls in, wrapping her arm around Roo's shoulder, the rest of the girls following.

"Call me Rupert," said Mr. Beckinsale.

"Cor Blimey," said Ruby tapping one of the other ladies on the shoulder, "I'm on first name terms with them upstairs."

Sitting down before a great, old, plank table, the girls waited as Ruby and her two kitchen staff hurriedly prepared them their late lunch. Whilst they did, the girls spoke in hushed tones of how they proposed to slip away during the afternoon to find the secret door. It was decided that Willow would go first unaccompanied; Mr. Beckinsale in his perpetual state of excitement would surely not miss just one of them. If she did not return in a timely manner, two of the remaining six girls would go looking for her, and so on. The original idea was that Mr. Beckinsale would take pity on the girls and send them to the cafeteria where they could discuss their plan openly. However, after eating Ruby's famous stew and dumplings, the girls were glad he hadn't. Thanking Ruby and her two staff, they made for the door but were interrupted by Ruby herself. Her face, in stark contrast to her usual ruddy 'been in the steam of the kitchen too long' complexion, turned pale and then paler still.

"You ought to be careful you young ladies, messing around in this 'ouse," she said in a grave and fretful tone.

"What do you mean Mrs. Hatchet?" enquired Willow, as if she was ignorant of all the mysteries attached to Horseforth.

"Well Miss I can't say as I don't know your pretty face and who you are."

Willow stiffened.

"Do go on," she said, trying without success to conceal her curiosity.

"Well Miss, you're Miss Portia of the Forbes Hamilton family aren't ya dear?"

"You know this, how?" enquired Willow.

"Well dear, I've been in the service of your family all my life, my mother before me and her mother before her. I knew of your existence of course, and even saw you when your father used to bring you to the 'ouse as a nipper. But I recognise you as you are now from your picture in the West Denton Chronicle. You remember, when that reporter came up from the 'smoke' to investigate the curse on Sutton some time ago."

"What's the smoke?" asked BB with a quizzical expression.

"That's the name given to London during Victorian times me dear, 'cause of the industrial pollution 'anging about in the air," answered Ruby.

"Anyhow Miss Portia, that's how I knows ya pretty face as it is today.

If it's anyfing to ya Miss, I never fought you were a witch or anyfing like, just a sweet, refined, young lady from a family, as like."

"Thank you, Mrs. Hatchet," said Willow sweetly, clearly touched by Ruby's sentiments.

"If I may ask Miss," Ruby continued, "did the article cause you much 'eartache me dear?"

"Willow fell silent for a little while, forming her reply carefully before speaking it aloud.

"Well Ruby," she began "yes it did. I was forced to leave my school and attend The Stanley in Sutton Althorpe. After the article appeared in the Chronicle, I was apparently thought to be a witch.

Although I bore it well enough, it was the Headmaster who requested I leave. He *assured* me however, it was my well-being he was concerned for."

Rubbing her hands clean on her apron, Ruby made towards Willow and embraced her.

"Dear girl, you aint no more a witch than I am a lady," she said kindly.

Strangely, for all she was haughty, Willow seemed very at ease in Ruby's strong and well worked arms.

Separating from her, she spoke.

"Mrs. Hatchet, I have been afforded every luxury and opportunity you can imagine, moving amongst the wealthiest and most influential of people.

You, however, are worth ten of the so called 'ladies' I have ever met."

Ruby's eyes turned watery and when she did speak her voice altered from gravelly and loud, to soft and somewhat shaky.

"Bless ya dear."

"Besides," said Willow brightly, "had I not been asked to leave The West Denton School, I would not have met my new friends." Before leaving the kitchen, Willow introduced Ruby to the rest of the Super Girls, after which they made their way to the afternoon's assembly point.

Later, whilst Mr. Beckinsale was marching the group from one room to another, Willow seized the opportunity to slip quietly away. Retracing her steps through the vast resplendent house, she prepared herself to confront the secret doorway, which, if Wasp was right, lay only a flight of stairs away. Gingerly, Willow clasped the great, wooden, banister rail that flanked the open side of the staircase and began to slowly descend it. As she neared the last few steps to the landing where the stairs turned the corner, it stood before her, the secret doorway.

At least it was the door Wasp had insisted was there, even though Willow had no knowledge of its existence. However, she thought, if it didn't lead to somewhere magical, it would lead you into the grounds with a nasty bump on your head, bottom, or both for that matter. Pausing for a moment to gather herself, Willow drew a deep breath, folded her cold, clammy hand around the banister once again and resumed her descent. The boards beneath her feet creaked and groaned eerily. Though they had always creaked and groaned in the past, it sounded much more foreboding now.

Moments later she stood within arm's reach of the door, her head filled with thoughts of Horseforth's ominous history. As she slowly reached for the crudely fashioned, door knob, visions of her Great-great uncle Montgomery, Emily Louise, the old gypsy woman and Miss Hoskins spun around in her mind. Then, shaking her head defiantly, she said aloud, "what utter nonsense!" Closing her delicate, slender fingers around the doorknob, she pulled it forcefully towards her. Task completed, Willow found no nonsensical opening to the outside of the building, no secret closet or alternate dimension, only darkness. Half disappointed, yet relieved, she bit her lip nervously and reached into the blackness, a little at first and then by degrees, further still.

Nothing happened. Without resolution, Willow turned to leave. Pausing for a moment, she decided to try again. Her second attempt however saw a very different outcome; for suddenly and without warning she felt herself being pulled into a void. Indeed, such was the force upon her, Willow felt she may very well be turned inside out. With the sensation of falling feet first in a chute, she hurtled ever downwards through violent twists and heart stopping turns. 'How much faster could one possibly go?' was the only clear thought in Willow's head as she fought to maintain her breath. Finally, as if an eternity had come and gone, she came to an abrupt halt, spilling onto a floor of some sort in an undignified heap.

Quite where she had landed, she knew not.

CHAPTER 7

The Labyrinth

Rising to her feet Willow began to dust herself off, complaining indignantly. Looking around she tried to determine where she might be, but all that surrounded her was darkness. It was cold and damp too, the moisture by the sound of it was coming from water trickling down the walls. "Hello!" shouted Willow nervously and half-heartedly, but there was no reply, just the echo of her own voice fading quickly. She shouted once more, louder this time, but still she heard nothing, and nobody responded. Remembering a small, key chain torch she had been gifted by Geoffrey, Willow rummaged in her school blazer pocket until she found it. Taking it out, she flashed the feeble light in front and around her. Willow had been right about one thing, there was water running down the walls; the walls however, were like those you'd expect to find inside a cave. If this was indeed the labyrinth, it was not as she expected, though quite what she expected, she was unsure. Pondering whether enough time had passed for any of the other Super Girls to have come looking for her, Willow was soon acquainted with the answer. Landing noisily in a tangled pile behind her, as if shed from a lorry which had suddenly pulled off at speed, Roo and BB appeared. Startled by their arrival Willow leapt back, as did BB. Roo in stark contrast casually rose to her feet, dusted herself off and said in a matter of fact way, "never been on one of those before, where are we?"

"The labyrinth I think," Willow replied, "where are the others?"

"They'll be along soon I imagine," said Roo.

Only moments passed before Angel and Wasp were dispensed onto the floor in much the same fashion as the previous arrivals, then in quick succession Solo, but no Momo.

"Where's Momo?" asked Willow of Solo.

"I don't rightly know, we were together up until I reached into the secret doorway, now I'm here and she isn't," she shrugged.

"Well we can't just leave without her," said Roo.

"Where were we going anyway? asked Solo with a quizzical, almost confused expression.

"To find a way out of this place of course."

"Darling Roo," said Willow, "if this is the labyrinth as we think it is, then there is only one way to get out."

In the dim light of Willow's little, key chain torch, a numb silence fell among the six girls, broken only by the late arrival of Momo. Coming to rest on the floor in a similar manner to the other girls, she sprang quickly to her feet.

"I'm going to have to work on that landing," she said with a cheeky grin.

"Hi everyone," she added, as if nothing out of the ordinary was taking place.

"Really Momo," scolded Willow in the near darkness, "is it impossible for you not to be late to every, single thing?"

"Oh yes, sorry about that everyone, I forgot my hat, and I only got this one last week, it's the second one my mum has had to buy me this term."

"Do you think we might shelve the pressing topics of punctuality and millinery to focus on our current predicament?" Solo interjected.

Once again the group fell silent, as the seriousness of their situation began to sink in.

"Well we need to find a source of light," insisted Willow, attempting to inject some hope into their collective plight.

"Yes, Willow's right," agreed Solo, "we cannot do anything, if we cannot see anything."

The girls silently considered their options until Wasp broke in.

"There's a light," she said pointing at something, "there, there, look," she went on excitedly.

The girls turned their attention to a little orb of light, which, although no bigger than a tennis ball, threw its glow far and wide. It grew rapidly, illuminating everything in its path, leaving no one in any doubt, they were indeed in a cave of some sort.

What followed next however gave them no time for further discovery. When the intense ball of light reached Willow's eye level, it suddenly exploded outwards, engulfing the whole room in a blinding flash. Though the burst of light dissipated quickly, it was some moments before any of the girls were able to see clearly again. When eventually they could, they were met with a figure of a woman, enveloped in a luminous glow. While the spectre like figure was not altogether familiar, she was not altogether unfamiliar. The girls instinctively drew tighter together.

"Emily Louise!" cried Willow, her face turning almost as white as the glow that surrounded the mysterious form before her.

"Yes my dear," she replied in a shrill menacing voice, "it is I. You know me, don't you deary," she sneered in a slow considered way.

"Is this *The, Emily Louise?*" asked Wasp, barely capable of coherent speech. Before Willow could confirm Wasp's fears, Emily Louise broke in.

"Oh yes deary," she said, pointing menacingly at her, "I am *The* Emily Louise."

Wasp shrank back, Willow grabbed her hand.

"Don't be afraid Wasp, it is not you she wants."

"Indeed not," scowled Emily, "in fact the rest of you are all free to go, all except you," she thundered pointing to Willow fiercely, her long gnarled finger, snapping out like a whip.

"Join hands and in no time at all you'll be back where you were, as if nothing had happened and no time had passed."

Willow surveyed the rest of the Super Girls, all of whom had their eyes fixed firmly upon her.

"Go," said Willow in a resolute but sombre tone, "all of you go, this is my fate, not yours."

A brief silence fell between the two parties.

"Well?!" bellowed Emily, so loudly in fact the glow around her began to distort.

"I'm waiting, don't make me change my mind," she threatened gleefully. Breaking the silence, Roo walked the uncomfortably, short distance that separated Emily from the Super Girls. Willow insisted she come back but to no avail.

"You don't scare us," said Roo, with more confidence than she should have.

Emily flew into a rage, sparks flying from the glow surrounding her.

"Is that so," Emily sneered, "then you too shall spend eternity in my little temple of torment. Anybody else?" she snapped violently, clearly enraged by Roo's brazen dissent.

Momo then walked boldly across to where Roo was standing, after which Solo and Angel joined them.

Willow set forth, Wasp followed before she had completed her first stride.

Only BB remained. The other Super Girls looked over their shoulders; Roo, Solo and Angel gesturing for BB to join them. Emily seized her moment.

"So, it seems that your little group is not quite as united as you thought," she mocked, piercing Willow with a cold stare.

"Come child," said Emily, turning her attention to BB, "you shall return home, let the others live forever in torment."

BB slowly approached Emily, the other Super Girls parted to let her through. Roo was just about to admonish BB for being disloyal, but sensing this, Willow spoke.

"Leave her Roo, it is her right to leave us, it must be her decision."

BB took her last steps towards Emily, leaving the others in her wake. Emily's face lit up with this small but damaging victory within her grasp.

"Now child I will speak a verse, once you've repeated it, you shall be home. Listen very carefully. In the name of bad, evil and wrong, deliver me back to where I belong."

There was a silence, a heavy, thick silence. BB felt the eyes of all present upon her.

"Well child, your turn," spat Emily impatiently. BB took one last look at the rest of the Super Girls, their faces an assortment of disappointment, scorn, and astonishment. Turning to face Emily once again, BB opened her mouth to speak.

"Rain or shine whatever the weather, The Super Girl Seven stick together," she chanted.

Everyone present, including Emily Louise were stunned into silence. BB then turned on the ball of her foot and returned to the group, at which the Super Girls cheered and squealed with abandon. Emily flew into a violent rage, causing sparks to spit indiscriminately from her luminous veil.

"So be it," she bellowed, "I could dispense with you all in the flicker of an eye lash, instead I shall have the pleasure of watching every one of you tormented for all eternity."

With that she let out an eerie, spine chilling cackle. The glowing orb in which she had first appeared, engulfed the room once more, then vanished, taking her with it. The room, however, did not return to its former darkness, for on one of the cave like walls were three torches aflame, casting random shadows as they burnt. After a momentary silence, Solo spoke.

"What shall we do now?"

"Well, I imagine those three entrances to the labyrinth will have something to do with it," replied Willow pointing to them.

"Come," she said resolutely, "let us take the torches and have a closer look. I'll take the first, Wasp and Angel can follow me, Roo you take the next, BB and Momo can follow you, Solo, you take the last. Everyone hold the hand of the person in front of them, so we stay together at all times, agreed?"

The girls grabbed the burning torches from the damp, craggy, rock face and ordered themselves as Willow had proposed. Linking hands, they made their way over to the three narrow openings on one side of the wall.

Stopping there, they fell silent looking to Willow for a decision as to which one they should choose to enter.

"So, which one Willow?" asked Roo. Willow looked intently before her, knowing the wrong choice would almost certainly be their last choice.

Some moments passed.

"This one," she said pointing with complete certainty at the tunnel to the left.

"How can you be so sure?" asked Wasp fretfully.

Willow looked back at her.

"We are in the labyrinth Wasp, there are no certainties, we just have to trust our instincts and each other."

"Everyone ready?" asked Willow, looking upon the rest of the girls, their faces still but for the flickering, torch light, dancing upon them.

"Let's go then," she said resolutely, trying to make it sound like they had a choice, when really, they did not.

Through the entrance and into the rabbit hole they filed; their only light, the torches they carried, their only hope, each other. As they wended their way along, only the sound they made broke the eerie silence within, that and the noise of the water trickling gently down the inside of the cave's walls. A little more time passed or seemed to have, for who really knew anymore. Presently the cave opened out into a rough, cylindrical sort of chamber. The girls rested there for a little while, sitting on the floor in the glow and warmth the torches threw. They chatted for a time before Wasp broke in. "Shhh, listen everyone, can you hear that?"

A tense silence fell amongst the group as they strained to hear the noise evident to Wasp.

"Do you hear it now?" she asked, hopeful someone else could, lest she felt she was imagining things.

"There's nothing there Wasp," said BB in a dismissive tone.

"Like the secret doorway wasn't where I said it would be?" Wasp retorted.

"She has a point," said Roo.

Just as she'd finished speaking, the torch flames bent to the will of a breeze.

"There must be an opening not too far ahead," remarked Angel enthusiastically.

"Indeed, there must," agreed Willow, springing to her feet in mid-sentence.

"Then it's possible Wasp heard something?" suggested Momo.

"Come, let's go," said Willow, taking up one of the torches. With that the girls resumed their trek through the rabbit hole in search of where the breeze might be coming from.

As they forged on it grew stronger, creating a sound only Wasp could identify as distant rumbling. The girls hastened their pace, and though they had no idea what lay ahead, they were drawn to it all the same. The rabbit hole took a sharp turn to the left, then as it fell away steeply, a small dot of light presented itself, not more than a hundred yards away by Willow's estimation. Making their way as fast as conditions allowed, the light ahead grew larger and brighter. Scurrying towards what seemed to be an opening, a draft of hot air funnelled past them.

Then, quite without warning, Willow fell violently from view. Wasp's lightning reflexes allowed her to grab one of Willow's wrists but in doing so she too was taken to the ground. Willow let out a piercing scream which echoed around the huge, cavernous opening that the rabbit hole had evidently led them into. Spilling out onto a small ledge which Willow had tumbled over, the other girls scrambled to rescue her, for waiting below, far below, was a pit of molten rock. Roo quickly dropped to her knees, reaching for Willow's other wrist, which she held onto for all she was worth.

"Somebody hold onto Wasp's feet," screamed Roo, "mine too," she added. BB and Angel were best placed to take up this task and did so without delay. Momo and Solo hung precariously over the ledge to secure their grip on Willow's forearms.

"Ok," said Roo, "on the count of three, we'll all pull together." "Ready 1-2-3."

The girls began to pull amidst the heat billowing upwards. Willow dug her heels into the rock face to gain traction and lever off the surface. Slowly she began journeying upwards. With only a couple of feet to go however, the ledge on which they were all perched, began to crumble.

"Quickly!" exclaimed Roo.

Willow was unceremoniously hauled to safety just as light shot up from below, attesting to the ledge's demise.

Rising to their feet, the Super Girls returned to the sanctuary of the mouth of the cave to decide what to do next.

"We'll have to go back to try one of the other caves, I imagine," said Angel with disappointed resignation. Willow remained quiet as if sceptical that she had made the wrong choice.

"Well Willow, what say you?" asked Roo.

Moments passed, Willow was still confounded, to the point she had not heard Roo speak at all.

"Well Willow, what do you think, shall we go back?"

"I suppose," she replied, her tone and expression equally unconvincing.

Picking up their torches, now burning low, the girls readied themselves to retrace their steps. As they made off, Wasp imagined she saw something shiny out the corner of her eye. She walked hastily past the other girls lined up behind her ready to leave.

"Where are you going Wasp?" asked Solo.

"Look!" she said pointing across the abyss, getting dangerously close to the edge in her enthusiasm.

"Look! Look!" Wasp repeated excitedly, before anybody had time to ask what she was pointing at the first time.

"It's part of the urn!"

The rest of the girls looked at each other in puzzlement.

"How can you tell from all the way over here?" said BB disbelievingly.

"There is something there," said Solo, taking the few steps over to where Wasp was standing.

"It's part of the urn I tell you," insisted Wasp.

The rest of the girls drew alongside, Willow was naturally reticent to revisit the site of her near demise. After a couple of minutes musing over what the shiny object might be, only Wasp was able to conclude it was a piece of the urn. To prove this, she gave a description of the painted detail upon it and what part of the urn it was.

Willow quietly and discreetly drew her to one side.

"Darling Wasp, forgive me asking, but how is it that you can see that much, that far away in this half-light? it's not humanly possible."

"We trust your judgment Willow, and as scared as we all are, we have stayed with you probably never to return home again," Wasp replied gravely.

"It's like you said, this is the labyrinth, there are no certainties, we just have to trust our instincts and each other."

Willow was taken off guard by Wasp's certainty, and for the first time felt the full weight of the group's sacrifice.

Putting both hands upon Wasp's shoulders, Willow looked at her squarely.

"Very well Wasp, let us tell the others."

Turning back to the rest of the group, Willow spoke.

"By raising your hand who thinks we should try to traverse the abyss?" she asked.

To Willow's complete surprise everyone of the Super Girls raised their hand, even BB, eventually.

"Then we must find a way of bridging the gap, as it were," said Willow.

Returning to the mouth of the cave, they mused on the dilemma. Much time passed with no solutions forthcoming.

"I wonder what they're doing back at Horseforth?" BB wondered aloud.

"Not this, that's for sure," Solo replied. Still the girls pondered, looking for the most part like any other set of school girls but for being the unwitting guests of the labyrinth.

"This place was created to torment any soul or spirit trapped within it, isn't that so?" Momo interjected.

"How is that helpful?" said BB, who had grabbed a handful of pebbles and was tossing them lazily over the edge of the rock face.

"Let her speak BB," said Willow haughtily, for she was always haughtier when scorning something or somebody.

"Do go on Momo."

BB pulled her usual disdainful face and resumed her pebble throwing.

"Well," resumed Momo, "to my thinking, it would be far more of a torment knowing you had a minuscule hope of freedom, rather than absolutely none whatsoever. Therefore," she concluded, "we could conceivably escape."

Whilst Willow pondered Momo's observations, a very strange thing occurred, indeed, so strange was it, none of the girls could quite believe their eyes. One of the pebbles BB had thrown seemed to be resting in mid-air; it did not plummet into the molten void as gravity would dictate. All eyes became glued on the one little pebble either defying gravity, or better yet, was resting on something that couldn't be seen, but existed all the same. The girls all converged around BB.

"Throw another one," insisted Willow, "try to get it near that one," she said, pointing at the first pebble.

BB did what was asked of her, and as unbelievable as it seemed, that pebble too came to rest in mid-air.

"Quickly!" said Willow authoritatively, "everyone gather up as many pebbles as they can, pile them up next to BB."

"Who else has a good throwing arm?"

"Momo, you're in the netball team, can you help her, Roo might you too? the rest of us will keep you supplied."

Wasting no time, the throwers began throwing, whilst the gatherers began gathering. Some time passed, and with its passing came faint hope that Momo maybe right. Perhaps there was a possibility of escape from the labyrinth. After much frantic work, the girls stared in silent awe at the spectacle before them. Stretched from one side of the abyss to the other was what could only be described as an invisible bridge. Pebbles of all shapes and sizes peppered the divide, forming a causeway from one ledge to the other. Though whatever the pebbles were resting on wasn't flat, but dipped in the middle like a rope bridge of some sort.

"Who's going first?" Solo asked the inevitable question. A silence befell the group as the reality of having to walk across something that but for a few pebbles did not appear to exist, sunk in. Added to which, if the bridge didn't hold up, whoever was on it at the time would be sent plummeting into the molten rock below.

"I'll go," said Willow, "I got us into this."

"You didn't get us into this Willow," Roo quickly pointed out, "we chose to stay."

"Well it will be my way of showing good leadership," Willow replied.

"Very well," said Roo.

Willow quickly embraced the other girls, they wished her luck. Solo advised her not to look down. Taking a deep breath, she clenched her fists tightly and contorted her face in anticipation of the possible grave outcome.

As she was about to bring her right foot to bear on the causeway, Willow was interrupted by Solo clearing her throat loudly and purposefully. Pausing, she turned with a pinched expression on her face.

"On your hands and knees though," said Solo emphatically.

"I beg your pardon?" replied Willow with equal conviction.

Solo mimed the movement for her.

"Yes, I know what you mean," said Willow indignantly.

"Solo's right," interjected Roo, "you'll have better balance and you can feel your way as you go."

"But on my hands and knees?" protested Willow.

"Yes, just think of yourself as one of the maids at home, but without a floor cloth and polish," quipped Solo cheekily.

"It's not my fault we're rich," Willow pouted uncharacteristically.

"Just kidding," said Solo in her own defence, "trying to lighten the mood," she added.

Taking another deep breath, Willow crouched down with a distinct scowl on her face and made forth, bringing one hand to rest on the invisible surface before mirroring the action with the other. In her wake, she left her fellow Super Girls with what seemed to be a collective inability to exhale. Gaining confidence, she began to progress along nicely, soon finding herself more than halfway across the divide.

Heat billowed up from the molten rock below and flashes of light shot upwards at random intervals, illuminating the huge cavern. The temptation to look down was strangely almost too much to bear, but Willow was a disciplined girl, capable of great resolve. She fought the urge, keeping her eyes firmly fixed upon the opposite side she was fast approaching. As she completed the last few yards, Willow pounced onto the ledge clearly visible before her. With her heart pounding, it occurred to her that she hadn't taken a breath the entire crossing. Now in two minds, she could not decide whether to fetch the piece of the urn and go back to the others, or have the rest of the Super Girls join her. The one thing she was certain of, was that time was against them and they would be looking to her for a decision.

"Quickly BB, then you Angel," Willow yelled across the divide.

"One at a time, I don't think the bridge will bear anymore."

"Hurry! you must hurry!" she insisted.

BB began to cross the bridge, traversing it rapidly and faultlessly. Next was Angel, who though slower and more considered, crossed without incident too. It had remained stable enough to ensure the safety of three of them, but it pressed on Willow that things could and surely would change. Momo came over next, followed immediately by Roo. It was only when Wasp began her journey the pebbles slowly began to drop into the depths below. Whatever unnatural phenomenon had formed the causeway was now evidently starting to weaken. Wasp was faced with the unenviable task of crawling along a surface that not only couldn't be seen, but was also disintegrating beneath her.

In the middle of her passage, she suddenly froze, then to further complicate matters, looked down. Becoming dizzy and unsteady she communicated her movements to the bridge beneath her, causing it to sway about.

"This doesn't look good," said Willow, her tone befitting the seriousness of the situation. That bridge is about a minute or two from collapsing," she added most assuredly.

"How do you know?" asked Roo.

"I just do," Willow replied. "One of us will have to go back and get her."

"But you said the bridge won't hold two of us at once," protested BB.

"If someone doesn't go soon, the bridge will be gone, taking Wasp with it and leaving Solo on the other side forever," Willow countered.

"Who weighs the least?"

"Momo," chorused Roo and BB.

"Momo, will you go and get her?"

"I'm a Super Girl aren't I?"

"You'll have to run though, crawling will take longer than we have."

Within seconds Momo started back on the bridge she had already once escaped the danger of. The pebbles that had guided her way the first time were now disappearing before her eyes, time was running out, and fast. Upon reaching Wasp, Momo grabbed her by the hand and pulled her unceremoniously to her feet. Running frantically to safety, Momo's leg suddenly slipped through the invisible surface. Wasp turned to help, but Momo yelled at her to carry on. Whilst she continued to run, Momo struggled to break free. On the opposite side Solo stepped onto the remnants of the bridge, but had only seconds to cross it by Willow's estimation. She ran clumsily, treading where the remaining stones still lay on the surface. Momo continued to struggle, causing the bridge to swing around violently.

The rest of the Super Girls looked on wide eyed and powerless to assist their two friends. Finally, Momo managed to slip her bonds. Seeing this was so, Solo picked up as much speed as she was able and prepared to make a grab for her on the way by.

As the pebbles began to cascade downwards like rain, she stretched out her arm, clenched Momo's hand and wrenched her towards safety. Landing on the ledge, their hands still fused to each other, Solo made it to the other side. Momo however, dangled precariously over the edge. BB and Roo lent over to grab her free hand, as they did saw the last of the pebbles disappear into the fiery void. One last pull saw Momo reunited with the flock, a few seconds less however, would have seen an entirely different outcome.

After a few moments spent in silence, Willow rose to her feet and made her way over to the piece of the urn that lay partially imbedded in the rock face. One by one the rest of the girls gathered around to see if their efforts and courage had yielded any result. Willow began digging gently around the piece with her hands, Roo bent down to assist and because the rock face was surprisingly soft, it wasn't long before the treasure was free. Holding it aloft, the girls studied it, passing it around for each other to look at individually.

"It's not very spectacular, is it?" exclaimed BB, pulling a face.

"We did all of that, for this?" she huffed.

Willow snatched it back from BB, raising her eyes indignantly.

"It matters not whether you appreciate it as an historical artefact BB, the point is, it's part of the key to getting out of here," said Solo scornfully. There was a brief pause as the group quietly gathered itself.

"Where to now Willow?" asked Roo, as she, like the rest of the group were faced with another three rabbit holes from which to choose.

"Oh great, another cave adventure," complained BB, who might as well have said nothing for all the notice that was taken of her.

"Oh no!" exclaimed Angel, suddenly realising something was awry.

"We have no torches."

"She's right," remarked Solo "we don't, we left them on the other ledge."

"We won't need them," said Willow confidently.

"Why is that?" asked Solo.

"I cannot say, just a feeling. Everybody ready? let's take the middle tunnel," and with that the girls filed one by one into the darkness, or so they thought.

CHAPTER 8

The Hall of Mirrors

Moments later the Super Girls found themselves in a room similar to the great ballroom at Horseforth Manor. Huge mirrors lined the walls, stretching just shy of the ceiling. Reflected in them, beautiful crystal chandeliers, ablaze, perhaps left on in anticipation of a visit? The floor resembled a deep black frozen lake. It was so shiny in fact, it looked as if you would slip over on it, or worse still, fall through it.

"Are we back at Horseforth?" asked Wasp innocently, not fully recovered from her walk across the invisible bridge.

"No," said Angel, taking up Wasp's hand to comfort her against certain disappointment.

"How do you know for sure?" enquired BB.

"No windows," replied Solo and Roo simultaneously.

BB took a second look, "no there aren't," she remarked with a look of perplexity.

"How odd, it's like one of those pairs of pictures where you have to spot the differences."

"This is still the labyrinth alright," said Willow, her tone grave and resigned.

"Well," she continued a little more optimistically, "what say we set to work?"

"How do you mean?" asked Wasp, a wrinkle forming above her brow.

"The second piece of the urn," replied Willow, as if surprised even Wasp had asked such a question.

"Oh of course," said Wasp, "absolutely."

"But where could you hide it in here? the place is empty, no cupboards, no shelves, nothing," BB observed.

Suddenly! there was a loud bang, which seemed to come from behind where the girls were standing. All of them shot their heads around, startled by the sudden intrusion upon the silence.

"What's that?!" panted Angel, her face pale with shock. Roo took the initiative to investigate first, walking in the general direction of where the noise seemed to originate. The rest of the Super Girls followed in short order, gathering near the site they entered the room.

"Look!" said Angel," the opening we came through, it's gone." Reaching out, she ran her hands over the wall, but there was no evidence of it ever existing.

"Perhaps the second piece of the urn is behind one of these panels?" suggested Solo, tapping at one to see what sound it would make.

"Seems pretty solid to me," said Angel.

"Yes I think you're right," agreed Solo.

"We'll have to go around the room, see if we can't find a hollow spot," said Willow.

"I'll go to the right with Angel and Solo."

"BB, Momo, Wasp and Roo you take the left."

"What if it's hidden higher than we can reach?" asked Angel.

"We will have to go around again on each other's shoulders or something," said Willow dismissively.

"Anyway, we will cross that bridge when we come to it."

In response to her comment the rest of the girls looked upon her searchingly.

An awkward smile crept over Willow's face.

"Perhaps that wasn't the best expression to use," she conceded.

Moments later, the ballroom came alive with the sound of knuckles tapping at its walls, not an altogether pleasing sound but necessary all the same.

As they progressed slowly and hopefully along, their knuckles became red and sore from continuous use. BB turned around, suggesting to Willow they rest for a few minutes. Glancing over, her attention was stolen by a red velvet pillow lying on the centre of the floor.

"*Willow, Momo, everybody!*" BB exclaimed excitedly, "*look! Look!*"

The girls shot around to look at what BB was so excitedly yelling about, and pointing to.

"It's another piece of the urn," she announced, hastily making her way towards it.

"*No! BB no!*" hollered Willow, with altogether more volume than anyone thought her capable of. BB came to a sudden halt, as if she had run into a plate glass window that had resisted her charge.

"Go back to the others," insisted Willow in her softer, less haughty voice.

"Let us meet in the middle of the back wall."

The two sets of girls filed back from whence they came, the air thick with anticipation. Arriving at the assembly point Willow had described, all eyes turned towards the centre of the room.

"That wasn't there before... was it?" said Wasp referring to the seemingly innocuous pillow on which a piece of the urn sat.

After some moments of incoherent mumbling, it was agreed nobody had seen it when they'd entered the room.

"How then, did we not see it materialise?" wondered Solo aloud.

"The bang!" exclaimed Momo excitedly, causing Wasp, BB and Angel to yelp in surprise.

"What?" enquired Roo, looking a little bemused.

"The bang... you know the loud noise we thought came from behind the wall.

We were distracted after that, otherwise we'd have been sure to see it."

"Momo's probably right," said Solo.

Why didn't you want me to just go and get it?" asked BB of Willow.

"It's too easy BB, I feel sure the labyrinth will not surrender a piece of the urn so cheaply."

"Yes BB," said Solo, supporting Willow's position, "look how perilous it was to acquire even the first piece of the puzzle. I can only imagine that every next one will get harder and harder to obtain."

"What shall we do then?" asked Roo.

"Well, I think the least that could happen is the chandelier might fall on whoever's beneath it, should we get that close," remarked Angel."

"Why don't we throw something under it?" suggested BB, "then if Angel's right, no one will get hurt."

The girl's fell silent for a couple of moments whilst they considered BB's suggestion.

"It's not a bad idea," said Momo, augmenting her opinion with a slight nod of her head.

"Considering the hall is twice as long as it is wide, we should probably attempt it from the side of the room though," reasoned Solo.

Following her suggestion, they converged at the closest point to the pillow.

"What will we throw?" asked Willow upon their arrival.

"How about I bundle up my blazer?" suggested Momo, removing and securing it by means of her school tie.

"Anybody?" she asked, offering it around to the others.

"No, you do it," said Willow "you have the arm for it."

"It would help to get a few steps closer."

"Very well, but we will all come with you," Willow insisted.

"Gingerly the seven girls made their way out on to the shiny, black marble floor.

After only a few steps, Willow gave the command.

"Stop!" she said firmly, feeling another step could end in calamity.

The Super Girls came to a sharp and precise halt.

Clutching the ragged projectile tightly, Momo withdrew he arm. As it passed her face on its return journey, she relinquished her grip on it.

The whole operation was executed like an Olympian making their last attempt for a gold medal. The untidy bundle spun through the air, never once looking as if it wouldn't reach its target. Seconds later it came to rest with a dull thud, kissing the cushion on which the piece of the urn was nestled. There was a palpable silence whilst the girls waited for some catastrophic event to take place, but nothing did.

"Great throw Momo," said Roo, beginning a round of applause, "indeed," said BB haughtily, poking fun at Willow, so Willow pulled the BB face to poke fun back.

"So you think it's safe to go over now Willow?" asked Roo, ever anxious to press on.

"Yes, but we'll all go together."

"Who's going to pick it up?" asked Solo.

"Who wants to?" asked Willow, surveying the group.

"I'll do it if no one else wants to," said Roo, after which no other offers were forth coming.

"Ok, Roo it is then," Willow announced, "let's go."

The girls tentatively resumed their passage across the floor, never leaving each other's side. At least this held true for six of them. BB wandered off to the far end of the hall and had begun carefully examining a huge mirror that stretched almost the entire height and width of the room. In her absence, Roo knelt down to retrieve the second piece of the urn. The rest of the girls stood in silence, waiting for something catastrophic to happen, but again nothing did.

Roo raised herself up with the piece in hand. Willow took the other they had, and offered it up to see if it would fit, and it did!

The Super Girls cheered and embraced each other with excitement, in that moment realising BB was missing.

"Where's BB?" asked Wasp, her face stricken with fear, imagining perhaps she had disappeared or been mysteriously taken from them by some other means.

"There she is," said Angel pointing to the end of the room.

"BB," she yelled, her voice echoing around the vast expanse.

But BB didn't even look up, instead she continued examining the mirror before her.

"Let's all shout," said Solo, so they did, but still BB was oblivious.

"She's playing a trick on us," said Angel, "I'll go and get her."

Angel made off, but after taking only one or two steps, a thunderous noise shook the whole room sending her to the floor. Roo and Willow suffered a similar fate. Momo, Wasp and Solo however had managed to brace themselves against each other and kept upright.

"What was that?" stammered Wasp.

As she spoke, another rumble thundered around the room, this time louder and more forceful than the last.

"Stay on the floor," yelled Willow to the other five girls, all of whom had now been spilled upon it.

BB remained at the other end of the room, graduating from staring at the mirror to poking at it.

"What an earth is she doing?" Solo asked, not expecting anybody to have more of a clue than she herself.

"I don't know," said Willow, "at least she's still upright. Let us try and make our way over to her." Another rumble came from beneath the floor, though this time it did not peter out like the last. Within seconds it began to vibrate as if something was churning beneath it. Just as quickly, a crack appeared across its entire width. The crack rapidly graduated to a gap, leaving Momo, Willow, Angel and Roo on the side of the room they entered, Wasp, Solo and BB on the other.

"We have to get out of here," Willow yelled above the tremendous noise that enveloped them.

"Where will we go?" shouted Solo, as the gap continued to widen.

Stricken with fear, they searched each other's faces for inspiration. Now the decision to be on one side of the floor or the other became two-fold; one of loyalty, the other survival. As the seconds passed, so too did the growing distance between them. From within the forming crevice a vortex made its presence felt. Making an executive decision, Solo decided it was time to act.

Bracing against the strengthening current, she and Wasp joined hands, closed their eyes and prepared to leap... Suddenly BB came running up from behind them, *"Stop!!!"* she yelled, startling them both.

"Willow, Momo, Roo, Angel, all four of you *jump! jump now!"*

BB screamed from her position opposite them.

Having absolutely no time to question BB's frenzied appeals, Willow took charge.

"Let's run back a few yards," she yelled. The girls hurried back at Willow's command, joined hands and counted down from three. Then with their eyes closed and their hearts pounding, they started to run.

Time seemed to stand still as they travelled over the vortex, until they were re-acquainted with its passing, hitting the cold, unforgiving floor beneath them.

Staying crouched low, they looked across at Wasp, Solo, and BB clinging onto each other.

"Quickly, quickly follow me!" screamed BB, moving as fast as she could towards the mirrored wall. With the floor continuing to withdraw, they blindly followed BB into the unknown. They forged on, not remembering the room to be as vast as it now seemed. The vortex strengthened, systematically devouring mirrors, chandeliers and even the parts of the ceiling to which they were attached.

Crawling the last few yards to the end wall, BB singled Wasp out and thrust her head first towards the mirror before them. With everything else going on it was hard to gauge what shocked the rest of the Super Girls most. Was it that BB had thrown Wasp bodily at a mirror, or, that Wasp had disappeared through it seemingly without a scratch?

"Now everybody else, go!" yelled BB, "go!"

One by one, like lemmings off a cliff face, the Super Girls disappeared into the mirror. Willow looked strangely reticent and seeing that she was faltering, BB grabbed her hand and they dived at their reflections with only inches of the floor remaining.

CHAPTER 9

Home?

Tumbling down a low, grassy bank, Willow and BB came to an abrupt halt courtesy of Roo and Momo. Both parties startled by the collision rose quickly to their respective feet.

"Momo, Roo?!" exclaimed Willow, breaking into nervous laughter at the sight of them and the rest of the Super Girls. They too reacted similarly.

After their collective relief dissipated, they sat on the grassy embankment they had tumbled down, trying to determine where they were.

"We're back in Sutton Althorpe," squealed Wasp excitedly, jumping to her feet and skipping merrily about.

"We're home! we're home!" she cried.

"That was some adventure," said Angel, seemingly excited it had happened, but relieved it was over.

"I'm going to join Wasp," she said, and no sooner had she spoken, she was gone, running down the hill with her arms out to her side, dizzy with relief.

"I think I'll join them," said BB, and off she went.

"Did *that* just happen?" asked Roo with a puzzled look upon her face.

Willow said nothing; instead she rummaged around in her satchel, presently producing a piece of the urn.

"Momo?" she then said, looking at her expectantly. Momo didn't respond immediately, causing Willow to panic.

"Tell me... you do still have it... don't you?"

There was a brief pause in which fear etched itself upon Willow's face.

"Oh yes, yes, of course," said Momo, after some tense moments.

"Upon my word Momo, you scared me half to death," Willow declared, pressing her palm to her chest and exhaling audibly.

Momo then produced from her blazer another fragment of the urn, carefully placing it beside the piece Willow had in her possession.

There was a brief silence whilst Roo examined the two fragments.

"Fair enough," she said matter-of-factly, satisfied beyond explanation, that, '*that*,' had, actually just happened.

"I don't understand," said Solo, a crease forming between her eyebrows.

"If there are seven pieces of this urn and we must recover all of them to get out of the labyrinth, why are we back in Sutton Althorpe after only finding two?"

"We're not," answered Willow swiftly and bluntly, allowing no false hope by even the briefest pause.

"What do you mean?" pressed Solo.

"Look around you," Willow continued, "over there's the Cooper's Farm, further down the hill, the village, and look beyond the trees, there's the church."

"Yes," agreed Roo, "everything is where it's supposed to be, don't you think so Momo?"

"It looks fine to me, though it feels a little strange."

"How so?" asked Willow, who already knew but wanted Momo to arrive at her own conclusion.

Momo paused to think.

"It seems a little dead, almost lifeless."

"Exactly," said Willow.

"Look around you, nothing's moving, there are no people anywhere, no animals in the fields, no birds in the air."

"You're right," said Solo touching her finger to her tongue and holding it aloft.

"Not even a whisper of a breeze at this time of year, and look those clouds could be painted on they look so still," she continued, pointing to the sky.

So we're still in the labyrinth," concluded Solo, looking at Willow for final confirmation.

"I'm afraid so," she assured her.

"But we do have these." reported Momo brightly, holding up the two pieces of the urn and smiling.

"Yes we do," conceded Willow, smiling back and throwing her arm around Momo's shoulder.

"Come, let us go and break the bad news to the others," she continued.

The four girls rose to their feet, wandering down the hill to where Wasp, Angel and BB had gathered.

Once there, Willow broke the news to the three of them. Though they were disappointed, they were somehow unsurprised their adventure hadn't ended, and a sense of resolve descended upon the group.

"So where now Willow?" asked Roo, ever anxious to keep moving. Willow paused for a moment taking time to look around her, then breaking her silence she spoke.

"Down the hill towards the village," she answered, with the same kind of certainty that was now becoming her defining characteristic; that and her haughtiness of course. Without hesitation the rest of the girls followed her lead, starting down the hill in lines of two with Willow at their spearhead. Some minutes later they arrived at the trough of the valley. The Super Girls fanned out, taking on the look of outlaws from the Wild West, preparing for a gun fight. All around them was calm, not even a ripple broke the pristine surface of the village pond.

Presently they sat beside it, taking some comfort in the peace that enveloped them, ever mindful that it could, and probably would, change. A minute or two passed before Willow broke the uneasy silence that had settled over the group.

"BB, how did you know the way out of the hall of mirrors?"

"Thank goodness somebody asked," sighed Solo, clearly unburdened of the question racing around in her mind

"Yes BB, tell us, why don't you?" Roo chipped in.

BB's face flushed, and for a little while she remained silent, her gaze cast down.

"Well," she began nervously.

"Promise not to laugh," she added, as if suddenly feeling self-conscious.

"Of course we won't," said Willow on behalf of the group, "you saved our lives, why on earth would we laugh?"

"Well," BB resumed, "it was as if it called to me, the mirror that is, not out loud or anything, but I felt drawn to it. As I got closer I saw what was on the other side. It was no more than a window to me; then I touched it and realised you could pass right through it too."

"Why did you not say anything sooner?" asked Willow.

"I felt sure you would see what I saw, then realising you couldn't, I thought perhaps I was imagining it all.

In the end I either trusted my instincts or we'd all have perished, that's when I came for you and threw Wasp through it."

"We owe you our lives BB," said Willow earnestly.

"Well if we get through this, I feel certain that we'll all get a chance of saving one and others lives, don't you?" BB replied, gravely.

Her words hung in the air for some time, leaving an uncomfortable silence in their wake. Not even Momo piped up with some gem of optimism.

"Let's get going, shall we?" said Willow, sensing all too clearly the mood amongst the group was turning grey.

"Yes, lets," agreed Wasp, "this place gives me the creeps."

"Like the other places were so much more touristy," joked Solo.

The girls rose to their feet, Willow pondered for a split second and then set forth up the steep hill opposite the one they had just walked down.

"Where exactly are we headed Willow?" asked Roo.

"Up there," she replied resolutely, pointing to a very old, oak tree that had been hit by lightning many years ago, but had apparently survived. It was identical to the tree that existed in the real Sutton Althorpe. Though majestic in the summer, the old, oak now stood skeletal. From the bottom of the hill it looked like a giant antler rising from a mythical beast, its head concealed by the rolling landscape. As they tramped upwards, the leaves autumn had so carelessly discarded rustled beneath their feet. The indiscriminate noise they produced, comforting, against a backdrop that had been copied so exactly.

Willow drew to a halt, the rest of the girls followed her lead.

Her eyes narrowed as if she was concentrating on a thought. After a few moments she marched quickly to the brow of the hill and around to the other side of the old tree. Once there she pointed to a rounded opening at the bottom of the trunk about six or seven inches high. On close inspection, it was clear the old tree had indeed suffered the slings and arrows of the elements, burnt and scarred from its brush with nature's wrath.

"It's in there," said Willow, pointing at the opening. Bending down, she quickly removed her school blazer and rolled up the sleeves of her blouse. The rest of the girls gathered around as Willow made ready to forage inside the trunk to retrieve the third piece of the urn.

"*Wait!*" hollered Wasp, startling some of the girls in the process.

"How do you know it's safe to put your hand in there, how do you know there's not something or somebody inside waiting to pull you in?"

"Well there's only one way to find out isn't there?" replied Willow, kneeling down to investigate. Wasp's trepidation was evidently shared by the rest of the girls as they looked on, each with varying degrees of anxiety etched upon their faces.

Willow's hand slowly disappeared from view, followed by her wrist, and finally her forearm.

Foraging blindly around for some moments she found nothing, so she lay on the ground to utilise the entire length of her arm.

Some tense moments followed before her upper body began to jerk uncontrollably and an expression of terror beset her fine features.

"*BB, Wasp!*" she screamed, as it was them who were closest to her.

"*Help me! help me!*"

"*What is it Willow?! what can we do?!*" panted Wasp, her face drained of its colour, as was BB's.

"*Grab my legs, my legs!*" Willow screamed in a fit of panic.

Diving to the ground, Wasp and BB did as frantically requested of them, bearing down on their friend's limbs for all they were worth. Roo grabbed Willow's exposed shoulder, whilst Momo leapt over Willow to try and get a grip on the other.

By then however, it was too late!

Willow gradually withdrew her arm from the inside of the tree trunk, whilst the rest of the girls waited in fearful anticipation. They counted off one unharmed inch after another, until Willow's whole limb emerged intact. With the third piece of the urn firmly in the grip of her unscathed hand, she burst into uncontrollable laughter. There was a momentary pause before the jurors returned their verdict about her practical joke. BB was so incensed that she turned an indescribable purple, whilst the usually placid Wasp almost jiggled with rage. Roo's face broke into a grin as the two of them continued to vehemently scorn Willow for her antics, exciting further laughter from both Willow and the rest of the girls. Some time passed before BB and Wasp saw the funny side of the prank.

Once the laughter had subsided, the girls got around to the serious business of comparing the two pieces of the urn they had with the one just acquired.

"Has anyone noticed how foggy it's getting?" Angel remarked whilst they were doing so.

"There's a noise too," added Wasp.

"I can't hear anything," said Solo, "can anyone else?"

Once again it was only Wasp who seemed to be able to hear beyond the scope of any other normal human being.

After a few moments she was able to describe what she was hearing as sounding like 'rustling'.

"Perhaps someone or something is coming for us?" said BB.

"Maybe?" Willow replied softly, "let us keep quiet so Wasp can concentrate."

A little more time passed.

"I hear something now," Momo interjected.

"Yes," said Wasp "it's definitely leaves rustling, perhaps there's a breeze getting up,"

"But the fog isn't moving at all," Angel pointed out.

"She's right," agreed Willow, a look of concern passing over her face.

"It's getting nearer, whatever it is," said Wasp.

"Time we were leaving," said Willow resolutely, her tone turning serious.

"But it's so foggy," bleated Wasp "how will we find our way through it?"

"Willow will know where and how," said Angel, confident in the fact she would.

"We have to get back to the village, I feel sure of that, but the fog is as difficult for me to navigate in as it is the rest of you. How about you BB, can you see through it?"

BB began to scan about her, as Wasp and the other girls listened intently to locate the rustling sound.

"What do you suppose it could be?" asked Wasp nervously.

"Well if it was a breeze, we'd certainly be feeling it by now," Momo pointed out.

"No, it's not the wind," declared BB, who had turned her back on the group to look for a way through the fog.

"Turn around everybody, look!" she said, pointing at a large pile of leaves which had amassed without their notice. One by one they scurried enthusiastically towards those already gathered, compelled by an unapparent force.

Scared, yet fascinated as to what might be taking place the group stood transfixed, little knowing that they were wasting precious time. In short order the pile rose high above them, at which point a gentle breeze made its presence felt. As it blew, it did not, as one might reasonably expect, carry it off in all directions, instead it seemed to carve purposefully away at the mound.

Still mesmerized, the Super Girls continued to observe the phenomenon, as the invisible but deft hands of the breeze kept at their work.

Presently dying down, its purpose was finally revealed.

Left standing before them was the image of a man around eight feet in height, constructed solely of leaves. Where his eyes, nose and mouth should have been there were just dark shadows giving him an altogether menacing appearance. For a moment, neither of the two parties said or did anything. "Do you think he means us ill?" asked Wasp as she huddled close to Willow's shoulder.

"Well," said Roo, "I don't think he's here to help us with our homework."

A slight breeze sauntered about the scene giving the figure before them the appearance of movement.

Then without any warning! 'the leaf man' suddenly bolted towards the Super Girls, his great stride devouring the distance between him and them in mere seconds.

"Run!" shouted Willow sharply, "towards the village, follow BB and do not look back!"

Scattering like mice, the girls bolted down the steep hill, fanning out to make life more difficult for their pursuer. Such was the length of the leaf man's stride however, he would be almost impossible to outrun. Willow had a fair chance of escape with her long legs and natural speed. Wasp being much smaller and frailer, could not however, be assured any such hope.

Continuing to course down the hill the girls ran as fast as their legs would carry them. With the leaf man quickly gaining ground, Momo drew alongside Willow.

"I'm going to create a diversion," she panted, endeavouring to keep up with her.

"What are you going to do?"

"You'll see, meet me in the village hall with the others, watch for me out of the back window and be sure to leave the door open."

"No Momo! no!" implored Willow, reaching out to grab her arm, preventing her from doing what, she had no clue.

Momo fixed her gaze upon Willow, "you must trust me," she said, "now go."

Willow reluctantly continued on, whilst Momo broke off to the right and shortly thereafter, stumbled, falling to the ground. Immediately the leaf man saw what he thought was an easy target and changed direction. Shepherding the rest of the girls towards the village hall, Willow tried her best to explain Momo's plan whilst in travel. Back up the hill a little, Momo darted from left to right trying to shake off her pursuer. As the leaf man altered his course in pursuit of his prey, his body fragmented, quickly reassembling when resuming a straight trajectory. This little trick would buy Momo some time, but ultimately, she knew she would be caught eventually, if only because she had run out of breath. Down at the bottom of the hill the girls assembled one by one in the village hall. Tired and breathless they rushed to the back of the building, where there was a small window facing the hill they had just raced down.

Momo, still a long way from home, was losing ground to the leaf man who had grown wise to her tricks.

Faces pressed hard against the window, the rest of the Super Girls watched on in helpless torment as Momo's fate seemed to have been decided. Wasp, whose vision and hearing seemed to be getting more and more acute, covered her eyes as Momo's pursuer moved in on her. With one great lunge, the leaf man engulfed their fellow Super Girl.

Momo was gone!

"Wasp tell us what's happening," insisted Willow. Afraid her eyes had not deceived her, Wasp removed her hands from about her face. Reporting that Momo had in fact been engulfed by the leaf man, a sombre silence fell around the room. The girls turned away from the window, scarcely believing that one of them had been lost. Wasp kept a vigil however, not understanding why after taking Momo, the leaf man hadn't immediately turned his attentions to the village hall for his next victim. Still far up the hill, he seemed preoccupied with something or somebody. It was then she witnessed a sight that she could not believe. Not wishing to excite the other girls right away, she looked again, but still the picture remained the same. It was Momo, still alive and running, but periodically disappearing from view, rematerializing some seconds later. Every time the leaf man lunged at her she literally vanished, leaving him to spill helplessly onto the ground. If Wasp's eyes were not deceiving her, she felt sure Momo had a good chance of out running her pursuer now. Whilst the other girls mourned, Wasp concealed her excitement until she was certain Momo was home free.

"*Quick! quick everyone! it's Momo!*" exclaimed Wasp, running to the front door. BB, Willow and Roo revisited the window just in time to get a glimpse of Momo drawing alongside the building.

"*She's right!*" yelled Willow, barely able to contain her excitement.

With that Momo could be heard racing up the steps to the village hall's entrance, appearing through the double doors, left open for her as she'd requested.

"*Quickly! quickly!*" she gasped, "*shut the door, shut the door!*" but Willow and Roo had already done so.

Momo, almost unable to stop running, continued the length of the hall, eventually drawing to a halt only when she reached the low staged area at its far end.

"BB, Wasp, everyone, barricade the door with anything you can find," said Willow.

The girls frantically set to work, stacking up as many chairs and tables as they could in the short time they had to do so.

Meanwhile, Willow crossed the room to where Momo was sitting, dizzy knowing she had made it back to them safely.

"Dearest Momo, how on earth?"

Momo interrupted, "later," she simply said, still panting from her narrow escape.

"Now Willow, *think!* where to next?"

As Momo put her question, the leaf man dashed by the side window of the building making for the entrance. Willow called all the girls to the back of the room where she and Momo had been seated.

"What now Willow?" asked Roo, whilst through a gap between the doors and the floor, the leaf man could be seen pacing back and forth menacingly.

"I think will be ok in here for a little while," she replied.

"What if he knocks the door down or finds a way in?" asked Wasp shakily.

"He has no great strength Wasp," comforted Momo, "his trick is to engulf you in his leaves and stop you breathing. He can't do that if he can't get at you."

"But he will wait," said Willow gravely.

There was a momentary silence, then Willow suddenly exclaimed.

"The pond!"

"The pond?" repeated Roo with a bemused expression.

"What about it?"

"That's where we must get to," said Willow with her trade mark certainty.

"Then what?" asked Solo.

"We dive in."

"We what?" exclaimed Solo indignantly.

"We dive in," repeated Willow.

BB raised her hand

"We're not in class now BB, what is it?" snapped Solo.

"I can't actually swim," she said sheepishly, blushing as she spoke.

"Never mind, Roo will look after you, won't you Roo?"

"Of course I will."

"Look!" shouted Angel, pointing to the door, her voice strained, eyes and mouth wide open.

Whilst the girls had been engaged in conversation, they hadn't noticed a sudden wind had whipped up outside and was now blowing a steady stream of leaves through the gap under the door.

As it blew harder an all too familiar shape slowly started to take form.

"We have to leave immediately," said Willow," through the window, quickly."

The wind blew harder still, whistling eerily as it delivered the unwanted guest little by little into the room. BB hurriedly worked at opening the window latch, though it wouldn't yield to her efforts. As she continued to wrestle with it, the rest of the girls grew evermore anxious. Taking it in turns to have a go, none of them were any more successful than she.

Roo rushed to the back of the hall were the leaf man was gradually regenerating. Grabbing a chair that had been barricading the door, she hurried back.

"Step aside everyone!" she exclaimed, before launching it at the window.

Alas, though it shook violently, it did not surrender to the force. Roo tried again but to no avail.

"I'll have to take a run at it," she insisted.

"But that means you'll have to go near the leaf man," said Wasp, expressing the group's concern.

"I'll be quick," she said confidently.

Running back several paces, Roo took a deep breath. Holding the chair aloft, she let out a continuous yell and made her approach.

A couple of seconds later the window was no more, shattering and splintering loudly as if it were applauding Roo for her strength and determination.

The girls filed quickly through the opening, Wasp first, for she was the smallest and the least able to run fast. Angel was next, then BB, Solo and Roo. Willow stayed behind to shepherd the last of her flock through, but Momo was gone. Willow called frantically for her but there was no time, the leaf man was only yards away. Pulling her long form carefully over the jagged glass remnants imbedded in the window frame, she jumped onto the ground and began running immediately she made contact with it.

Catching up with the others, Willow shepherded the girls to the pond, sensing this would be the means of escaping into the next portal. The leaf man was in hot pursuit, closing in on Wasp at an alarming rate. Then from nowhere, Momo flashed across his path, so closely and with such speed, she briefly took some of his component parts with her.

Reassembling quickly, he altered his course determined to capture his quarry this time, bounding towards Momo whilst the others made good their escape. Arriving at the pond, Roo took

BB's hand and before she had time to argue, dived down into the water with her attached.

Angel and Solo followed next, then having seen that Wasp had taken the plunge, Willow followed her. Meanwhile Momo kept the leaf man occupied, morphing from visible to invisible. Seeing the rest of the Super Girls hadn't returned from beneath the pond's surface, she turned and started towards it. Desperately trying to exercise her new-found ability to disappear, pivotal to the rest of the groups escape, Momo was unsuccessful.

Seeking a conventional means of avoiding capture, she ran the last few yards to the pond, leaping in as the leaf man took one last desperate swipe at her. As Momo broke the gloomy surface an intense light revealed itself from the depths, which she instinctively swam towards. Looking back over her shoulder, she saw her pursuer meet his demise, reduced to no more than a thin blanket of leaves stretched across the water's murky expanse. She continued to close in on the brilliant light, drawn to its serene, watery glow.

CHAPTER 10

What Lies Beneath?

Momo found herself in a room surrounded by the other Super Girls, all of them suspiciously dry after their watery experience. As usual she was the last to arrive, though no one minded at all on this particular occasion, not even Willow.

"Where are we?" she asked.

"Some kind of auditorium by the looks of it," Willow replied.

Momo looked around, familiarising herself with the new surroundings.

Some five or six feet above the girls hung a ceiling that extended outwards along the sides and back wall of the huge room. Beyond that lay an enormous floor, fashioned from thousands of pieces of ceramic tile, no bigger than the palm of a child's hand. Depicted upon it were the images of five mythical looking beasts. Each corner displayed a fearsome, rhinoceros like creature with a head at each end of its body. The middle was dominated by a dragon like animal with a long neck and sharp looking fins cascading down its back. Its face was flanked with a spiky, reptilian like mantle, giving it a most fearsome appearance. At the front of the massive room there was a very high and equally magnificent stage area, on which a single grand piano sat dwarfed by its surroundings.

Shrouding the piano, from one end of the wall to the other, were beautiful, white curtains, ornately decorated with gold ribbon. The Mezzanine floor overhead had rows of seats upon it, terminating when they reached a honeycomb of private viewing boxes at the top. Stained glass windows handed off to the ceiling. So high were they above the huge, gilded chandeliers that lit the room however, it was impossible to see what was depicted upon them.

All in all, this was far more an imposing room than anything the girls had seen to date, even at Horseforth.

"Shall we venture out to get a better look?" suggested Roo in a whisper.

"Why don't we stay under the canopy," suggested Willow. "We don't seem to have much luck with open spaces, do we?"

"Good point."

"Let's make our way to the stage, shall we?" continued Willow in a lowered voice.

The group of girls threaded their way through tables and chairs that looked as if they had never been sat at, or on. Once at the end of the room they climbed a number of low stairs up to the stage.

"Wow!" remarked Wasp, rotating her head slowly around, surveying as much detail as she was able of the great room. The rest of the Super Girls gravitated towards the piano, on which stood a candelabra, as large as it was embellished.

As they neared, the candles perched perfectly straight upon it, sprang aflame.

The girls set back on their heels.

"Seems as if we are the guests," said Roo.

"Wait," said Willow, holding her hand aloft.

"I wonder if it works," asked Angel after some moments of silence.

BB wandered over, opened the lid and banged clumsily on the keys in no particular order.

"There you go," she said.

"You can play, can you not Willow?" asked Momo.

"Oh indeed I can Momo, in our family it's either that or be disowned," she informed her disapprovingly.

"Well let's hear you then," said Solo.

"Yes," chimed the rest of the girls in turn, except Wasp, who was off to the side of the stage still examining the surroundings.

"Alright," agreed Willow, "but only if Solo dances for us."

"Yes Solo," said Momo "that's fair."

"But I haven't got my blocks or even my shoes," she protested.

"Then dance in your socks," said Momo, clearly not wishing to be disappointed.

"Ok, ok," Solo agreed.

Whilst Solo made ready to dance, stretching and contorting herself in every which way, Willow prepared to play.

She pulled from under the piano a beautiful shiny bench that on its top had a thick tasselled cushion, matching the curtains. Willow flexed her long, slender fingers and sat upon it. Meanwhile, Solo ran out onto the floor as if every chair and box in the auditorium were occupied. Positioning herself, she waited for Willow's cue.

"What shall I play for you?"

"Do you know the Dance of the Sugar Plum Fairy, from The Nutcracker?"

"Indeed I do."

"Then that it is," said Solo.

Presently Willow began; the beautiful sound of her piano playing resonated throughout the great room, wrapping itself around every corner, curve and surface.

Solo for her part took on the look of a fairy as she glided silently around the magnificent floor; she and Willow's piano playing were as one. The rest of the Super Girls scattered about the stage, though none of them very far apart from each other. None of them except for Wasp, who to anyone looking on displayed a greater interest in the architecture of the room, than the ballet or piano that was being performed in it.

Whilst Momo looked on at the spectacle produced by the skilful union of Willow and Solo, she caught Wasp's eye. Taking full advantage of this and not wanting to break the calm that had settled over the group, Wasp subtly beckoned her over. Surmising Wasp was concerned about something, Momo quietly slipped over to her vantage point and sat beside her.

Wasp looked nervous, even more nervous than usual.

"Momo," she whispered sheepishly, "I saw how you escaped from the leaf man."

Momo didn't answer straight away, only having an inkling of how she'd achieved it herself.

"What did you see?" she asked, not wishing to give any clues in her reply.

"I saw you disappear, then reappear; though when you weren't visible, it was more like you were able to blend in with your surroundings. How did you do that?" asked Wasp, with a look on her face that would give you to believe she was unsure she really wanted to know.

"I cannot tell you Wasp, only that I felt I'd be the one to get us away from the leaf man. I knew not how, though I also knew I couldn't outrun him."

There was a brief and awkward pause, eventually broken by Momo.

"Now Wasp," she resumed, "how is it that you saw what you did when none of the others could?"

Wasp looked somehow guilty, as if she had been discovered

doing something wrong, but before she had time to reply Momo spoke again.

"How is it you can see and hear way beyond anything the rest of us are capable of, or indeed, any other human I should think?"

"I have been wondering about that."

"What's your conclusion?" Momo asked searchingly.

"I will tell you, but now is not a good time."

"Why not"? Momo asked with a quizzical expression.

"Look up there," said Wasp, subtly pointing to the stained-glass windows at the top of the walls. Momo's eyes followed the direction Wasp was pointing in.

"I see the coloured glass but no more detail than that."

"What do you see?" Momo asked, both anxious and eager to know.

"Those pictures in the glass, they're not just decorative, they tell a story. As you follow from window to window, the story unfolds."

"Go on."

"Before I do, I must ask if you can disappear yourself at will? do you have that much control over this power of yours?"

"I cannot say," replied Momo earnestly.

"Whilst the others are preoccupied, could you perhaps try?"

"Ok."

Composing herself Momo concentrated hard, her eyes glazing over as if she was asleep with them open, but nothing happened.

Momentarily she looked sideways at Wasp, only to be met with a disappointed expression.

"I'll try again," she said resolutely.

Again, Momo focused her efforts and thoughts, but again nothing happened. Wasp's face dropped, as if it were she who could not summon her power.

"Don't worry," said Momo, putting her arm around Wasp to console her, "at least you have your special power."

"That's just it though Momo, perhaps I don't have this very acute sight and hearing, but merely imagine I do."

"No, no," Momo petitioned, "you haven't been wrong so far. Remember the urn over the other side of the abyss, the noise you heard long before any of us."

"But then how about what I saw of you, or thought I did?" Wasp countered.

"Momo's concentration was momentarily broken as she quickly put her hands about her face. Tilting her head back, eyes flickering, she sneezed.

"Forgive me Wasp," resumed Momo, gently rubbing the water from her eyes caused by sneezing. Seeing clearly again she was greeted with the biggest smile she had ever seen on Wasp's face.

"You did it Momo, you did it!" exclaimed Wasp with all the excitement a whisper would allow.

"Did what?"

"That thing, the disappearing thing, first you were going to sneeze, your eyes flickered then you were almost gone."

"Almost?" enquired Momo playfully.

"Well you didn't disappear entirely, just sort of became translucent."

"Try it again, this time though close your eyes," said Wasp excitedly.

Momo composed herself, gradually letting her eye lids fall until they were completely shut.

Wasp looked on apprehensively.

Presently Momo's image faded, slowly at first, then in a second, she was gone. Wasp looked on in silent awe at the empty space Momo had occupied only moments before.

Reappearing, she was greeted by Wasp's beaming smile.

"Oh my," she said, putting her hands to her mouth, stifling her excitement.

"Did it work?" asked Momo eagerly, sensing it had.

"Oh yes, yes indeed it did!"

"Now, tell me, about this story on the windows up there?" asked Momo, subtly casting her eyes skywards.

Wasp's face fell, her smile evaporating like a solitary raindrop on a hot day.

"What's wrong?" said Momo, taking up Wasp's hands in hers.

Wasp paused for a moment and then begun.

"The first pane of glass is an image of this very room, including rough depictions of the beasts on the floor. The second depicts people making merry. The third..." Wasp paused, her complexion turning pale, her hands clammy.

"Yes... and the third?" prompted Momo.

"The third shows the floor erupting, the images of the beasts that have been walked upon, coming to life."

"In the fourth picture, all of them have been awoken, the two headed ones protecting the giant in the middle.

"The fifth..." Wasp looked at Momo squarely, pausing ominously.

"The fifth... all of the peopled dead, the room almost completely destroyed except for the walls."

"What of the fourth piece of the urn?" asked Momo after a few moments spent in silence.

"I was coming to that."

Momo's grasp on Wasp's hands unconsciously tightened, as she prepared for the final instalment of Wasp's story.

"It's in the belly of the beast Momo... the big one!"

"So Solo is in mortal danger, and we have to go up against those," whispered Momo, nodding towards the stained glass windows.

"Yes, that's about the sum of it… and realistically you're her only hope, you're the only one who can distract them by disappearing and reappearing at will, as you did with the leaf man.

The beasts will soon rise, and Solo will never get away without you creating a diversion for her."

"What happens after we get her back, how will we tackle the beasts, and with what?"

"I don't know Momo, we'll have to think of something."

The music came to its end, whereupon the rest of the girls applauded. Solo stood hands on hips panting to catch her breath, many, many, yards from the stage area. As she made to skip back to it, Wasp bellowed at her to stop.

"Solo don't move!" she yelled, the sound of which echoed eerily throughout the room.

The rest of the girls were startled, not only by the ferocity of the voice but by the tiny figure from whence it came. With her hand held up in front of her, Wasp quietly but firmly impressed upon Solo to stand as still as she possibly could.

"Momo are you ready?" she asked.

Momo nodded, 'yes', though she looked pale and apprehensive, her cheeky smile abandoning her on this occasion.

"What on earth is going on?" asked Willow with a bewildered expression.

Wasp held one finger to her lips in a gesture for Willow to be quiet, adding "Shhh" to augment her point. She then made her way over to Willow, who was still at the piano with the rest of the girls assembled around her. As best she could, she tried to explain the events about to unfold. However, the girls would have to witness

Momo's new found power to believe it, so this she omitted. Wasp turned to Solo once again, who, as instructed hadn't even twitched, save the pounding of her heart through her blouse.

"Solo, nod if you can hear me clearly?" asked Wasp.

Solo nodded a 'yes'.

"Ok, very carefully start making your way to the side canopy, take the lightest and smallest steps you can. If you feel anything strange happening, run behind one of the pillars but keep off the beasts whatever you do."

Gathering herself, Solo took a deep breath and started forwards, tentatively bringing her weight to bear on *what lie beneath*. Wasp gestured for Momo to go and assist her as they'd arranged and then fell quiet. Momo walked over to the end of the stage, taking the steps back down onto the floor, knowing that if things went as Wasp had predicted, she would very soon need full control of her power.

Seconds passed, Solo had made a little progress in reaching her objective, whilst Momo began hers. Everything was looking good until from high above a gentle tinkling sound evidenced itself, fading quickly thereafter. Instinctively everyone looked skywards. Wasp discretely encouraged Solo to keep looking and moving forwards.

Turning her attentions to Momo, she closed her eyes as a signal for her to do the same. Momo nodded so she knew she'd understood.

"Now everybody, keep your eyes on Momo," said Wasp, sensing she was about to vanish.

Seconds later she was gone. The rest of the Super Girls were left speechless.

"How on earth…?" began Willow, who was so awestruck that she was unable to finish her sentence.

"Wow!" exclaimed BB.

"That's going to come in handy around Miss Hoskins," remarked Roo. The group's awe was quickly dampened by the return of the crystal chandeliers' deceptively sweet sound. As they swayed lazily overhead, their music grew louder and less enchanting.

"It's time," said Wasp decisively. "Angel, BB come with me, Willow, you and Roo wait for Solo to join you over the other side."

The two groups quickly filed down opposite ends of the stage and made their way under the canopy. Taking up positions behind the huge marble pillars supporting it, they waited. Dull, wrenching sounds replaced the music playing above them.

There was a momentary silence, almost too painful to bear, before the floor erupted, sending thousands of the tiles from which it was made, skywards.

Wasp shouted at Solo to run but she didn't need telling and was already heading towards Willow and Roo. A thick cloud of dust enveloped the room from inside which, a deep, gravelly, growling sound emanated. As the dust spread itself thinner, a large, monstrous mass appeared from behind its veil.

"What on earth is that?" exclaimed Solo, who, but for some quick footwork would have been face to face with it.

"That's the ugliest thing I've ever seen in my life," remarked Roo, "apart from Miss Hoskins," she quipped.

Meanwhile out on the floor somewhere, though no one knew exactly just where, was Momo. The beast began to prowl slowly and clumsily around the floor, sniffing out its prey as it went.

It appeared as depicted, three horns about its face, one on each side, the other protruding from its snout like a rhinoceros. The same head duplicated itself at the other end of its body, appearing as if someone had held a mirror to it halfway along its length. The thick, grey skin that covered the whole assembly moved so little it seemed to slow the beast's progress. The Super Girls knew if they didn't act quickly it would soon wander in pursuit of them, treading on its likeness and bringing another of its kind to life.

When Solo had danced, she had kept near the stage, only skipping upon the image of the beast now before them. If the story on the glass was true, each beast was only awoken when directly set foot upon. Though the room was vast, sooner or later it would be sure to wander on one of its counterparts, or worse, much worse, the giant in the middle. Momo suddenly rematerialized. Catching the beast off guard, it immediately began to lumber towards her, gradually gaining speed. Staying visible, she quickly altered her course as she had done with the leaf man. Then as the great lumbering beast closed in on her, she disappeared. Confused, it turned its attentions to BB, Angel, and Wasp. Sauntering menacingly in their direction it rasped and growled as it drew closer. The three girls spread out, none of them straying far from the marble pillars affording them protection. On the other side of the room, Willow, Roo and Solo were employing the same tactic, making it difficult for the beast to choose a victim.

Moments passed, the beast faltered as if confused. Suddenly, it thundered towards Willow, Roo and Solo, passing over a part of the floor she had not danced upon. Within seconds another of its kind was awoken, duplicating the destruction the arrival of the first had caused. Now there were two of them to contend with, but as a small consolation the charging beast had been distracted from its course by the appearance of the second. Working together the two hideous creatures set to their task, the first pursuing Willow, Roo and Solo, the new arrival lumbering back to the other side of the room to menace BB, Angel and Wasp. Setting its sights on Angel, beast two lowered its head and galloped clumsily across the floor, its large, dark, lifeless eyes fixed upon her. Darting behind the next pillar she evaded the attack, watching it slam into the stone column she had previously sought the refuge of. Such was the force of the impact it sent a crack coursing through the hard stone.

As the girls dashed from pillar to pillar, the great hall resonated with the almost rhythmic sound of destruction. The unrelenting charges of the creatures sent debris flying everywhere. Small shards of glass tinkled as they cascaded from the windows above and the massive chandeliers twitched with each new sortie. Whilst the beasts were doggedly trying to winkle the Super Girls out of their hiding places, Momo suddenly rematerialized in the spot the first beast had appeared in. Waving her hands and shouting to get their attention, they ceased menacing the other girls to focus their efforts on her. As they set up to charge, Momo slowly walked from the corner of the floor nearer to the centre, careful to stay a safe distance from the image of the great beast in the middle. Lowering their heads, the two animals thundered towards her, their great feet on the hard, unyielding surface beating out an ominous rhythm. The rest of the Super Girls looked nervously on as the gap decreased. Just as it had almost evaporated completely, Momo vanished, leaving them no time to alter their course. They cannoned into each other, one or both, letting out a deep agonised roar which filled the room. Beast two, fatally wounded, slumped to the ground like a felled tree, his counterpart, limped slowly away.

Momo reappeared under the canopy to the relief of Willow, Roo and Solo, who hugged her excitedly.

Sensing the full extent of its injuries, the remaining beast staggered over to the far corner of the floor to awaken another, falling unceremoniously to the ground thereafter. Whilst it let a sickly growl, the third of the four animals appeared, presenting every bit as fierce as its predecessors. Momo spirited away, reappearing dangerously close to her latest adversary. Immediately it set its eyes upon her and began to charge, whereupon she vanished.

She continued to bait it in this way for some time, tiring and confusing it.

Seeing she had the situation under control the other girls remained hidden, keeping as still and quiet as they possibly could, most of them at least.

Frustrated, the beast began to walk towards the canopy. Spotting BB, who insisted on fidgeting, it charged without warning, burying its great horn into one of the marble pillars as its counterparts had done. The other end of the beast spotted Willow, Roo and Solo and prepared to charge in their direction. After it had taken only a few steps however, the clumsy great animal paused. For some inexplicable reason it begun swinging both heads towards its abdomen. It was unclear why this was happening until fragments of rock could be seen bouncing off its torso.

Momo, who had chosen to stay invisible, had evidently come up with a new plan to distract the enemy. One after the other rock fragments flew into the creature's belly, and as they did it became increasingly ill-tempered. With such thick skin, all perhaps they could do was tickle, but it was evidently enough to distract it from its prime objective. As it grew angrier, it became increasingly more forceful, eventually impaling itself with its own horns.

With the three rhinoceros like creatures dispensed with, Momo reappeared, applauded by the rest of the Super Girls who knew it safe to come out of hiding. Meeting close to the middle of the floor they began to muse over how they could possibly retrieve the fourth piece of the urn. If Wasp was right, and she had been so far, it lay deep in the belly of the great creature depicted at their feet. A relative calm settled on the decimated room, save a few bits of debris still falling from the battered marble pillars. The calm however was short lived, as with a sudden crack, the main chandelier broke from the ceiling, hurtling towards earth, its giant chain trailing behind it. Like a comet with a fiery tail it coursed downwards, ending its short but spectacular journey crashing onto the centre of the floor. The girls quickly crouched low, shielding themselves from the hail storm of crystal shards raining down on them. When the 'storm' had passed over and the tinkling sound of flying crystal had abated, a twisted cage of metal was all that was left of the once resplendent object.

Though it was regrettable that something so lovely had been destroyed, it was certainly nothing compared to the significance of what it had fallen on.

"Oops," said Roo, only to be scowled at in complete disbelief by Solo, Willow and Angel.

"*Oops?*" repeated Willow perplexedly, her scowl seemingly cast in stone.

"Well you know?" appealed Roo. "I was just saying, it's unfortunate, that's all."

"Really Roo, that's the sort of inappropriate nonsense we expect from BB," admonished Willow.

The other girls grinned, BB frowned.

"Thanks a lot Willow," she retorted.

"I'm sure she meant it with affection," Momo consoled her.

"Can anybody else feel the ground rumbling?" asked Angel meekly, knowing that it was impossible not to.

"*Quick!*" said Willow "*run!*"

"Where to?" asked Solo.

"Good point."

"There's a door behind the curtain, next to the stage," said BB, pointing in that direction as the ground began to swell around them.

"That's of course if you believe a girl who talks nonsense," she said poking her tongue out at Willow.

"How do you know BB?" asked Wasp.

"I can see through the curtains, come, I'll show you."

As the floor continued to buckle and blister at their feet, resembling a disquieted ocean, BB hurriedly led the charge to the left of the stage at the end of the room. Arriving at the far corner, she grabbed the end of the curtain and thrust it aside, revealing, just as she had said, a door. Willow brought her hand to bear on its large black handle, faltering when it reminded her of the one at Horseforth. Casting such memories aside, she resumed the task of trying to open it.

"It won't open," declared BB.

"Why not?" asked Willow.

"It's locked from the other side."

Willow was about to speak, when she was interrupted by a sound so loud that it was as if the whole room had collapsed in on itself.

"*Quickly everyone!*" behind the curtain, stand as close to the wall as you can."

The girls followed Willow's instructions, a layer of fabric now the only thing between them and a torrent of flying debris. Amidst the shower an ear-piercing wail rang out. So loud was it in fact, the remaining chandeliers, clanked with the vibration.

"Stay perfectly still," said Willow "keep your backs pressed hard against the wall and stand on your tip toes."

"BB, can you see what's going on?"

"It's the big one alright," she replied, "and judging by his mood, I don't think he's very happy we woke him… and," BB paused before her next instalment of news.

"He's coming this way," she resumed.

Another roar echoed throughout the room, followed by the ear-splitting sound of glass splintering into fragments.

Willow looked at BB questioningly for further commentary on the beast's movements.

"Oh!" she exclaimed, after a few moments spent in ignorance of what Willow was silently trying to convey.

"That was the sound of him ripping one of the chandeliers from the ceiling and throwing it to the floor."

"He can reach that high?" asked Roo disbelievingly.

Actually he hit his head on it," BB reported matter-of-factly.

"Oh dear," said Roo dejectedly, wishing she hadn't asked at all.

Presently, yet another tremendous noise resonated throughout the vast room.

"What is it? what is it?" implored Willow.

"It's the last of the two headed beasts, I think the big one must have woken him."

"Oh no, wait a minute, *quickly, quickly, cover your faces!*" said BB in a panicked tone.

As Willow was about to speak, a shrill and desperate cry rang out, accompanied by a loud, deep roar that sounded like it came from the giant.

"Down everybody down!" screamed BB, after which came an enormous crash, followed by the random tuneless clatter of the piano as it slammed against the wall, causing the curtains to billow from the force. Pieces of it shot high into the air, falling some moments later about the stage. One of the fragments descended onto its stricken keyboard, hitting a high note that rung out defiantly

against its plight, causing Angel to shriek loudly with surprise. The room fell quiet, though it wasn't a serene quiet you'd be glad to experience, more the kind that precedes impending doom.

"What's going on BB?" asked Willow in a slow considered way, conveying she already knew, but wished not to.

"Do you want the good news or bad news first?"

"Really BB!" exclaimed Willow despairingly.

"Well then, the good news is the big beast has lost his temper to such a degree the last of the smaller ones is now dead."

"And the bad news?"

"Well..." BB paused, "he's coming this way," she continued shakily.

"I'll go and distract him," said Momo, thinking quickly.

Momo quickly made her way to the end of the curtains, disappearing herself before setting foot on the floor. Only the crunching sound of the devastation beneath her feet gave the great reptile any indication of her existence.

The beast soon became distracted by the presence he could hear but not see. Running around the back of him, Momo rematerialized, whereupon she began to shout and wave her arms about her. The great creature shot its head swiftly around, causing a plume of dust to shoot up from the floor.

"BB keep watching her, the rest of us will see if we can do something to get this door open," said Willow.

"Where's Solo?" asked Roo.

There were blank faces all around.

"She did make it behind the curtain," said Wasp.

"Who was standing next to her?" asked Willow.

There was a brief silence.

"Come on, come on, think!" rasped Willow impatiently.

"Oh I know!" exclaimed Angel.

"Yes, yes," demanded Willow, "who then?"

"She was standing next to Momo."

Willow exasperated, raised her eyes and tutted.

"What's happening with Momo, BB?" she asked, switching her focus.

"You may ask her yourself, here she is."

Momo appeared around the curtain's edge, having made herself visible just as she got to the stage area where BB had seen her.

"Did the giant see you come behind the curtain?" Willow asked worriedly.

"No he didn't, I flashed from invisible to visible, then back again quickly, knowing BB would be looking out for me. I didn't want to startle anyone lest they should give the rest of us away."

"Good thinking," said Willow, "what of the giant Momo?"

"He's busy, he thinks I'm under that pile of rubble, but I cannot hold him for very much longer."

Willow took up Momo's hand.

"Darling Momo," she began.

"What is it?" asked Momo, sensing all too easily there was something awry.

"Solo's missing. Angel said you were standing next to her when we were lined up behind the curtain, is this true?"

"Yes it is, but that's the last I saw of her."

Willow's face fell into an expression of both sadness and confusion.

"Well she can't have just vanished, said Wasp, "or can she?" she added, second guessing herself.

"I think your giant has had enough of that game," interjected BB, still keeping her vigil.

"What do you mean BB?" Momo enquired.

"Well he's starting to walk back this way."

The girls looked searchingly at each other, stricken with fear and bereft of ideas,

Roo broke the awkward silence.

"Can anyone else smell burning?" she asked, her nose twitching like a rabbit's.

"Look the curtains! the curtains have caught fire!" cried Angel, frantically pointing at smoke rising from the hems.

"The candles must have caught them when they fell from the piano."

"I think he's seen us," said BB changing the subject from bad to worse.

Willow turned to Momo.

"Do you think you can keep him busy a little longer whilst we try the door again?"

"Yes, I should think so, but do hurry."

Momo set to work, whilst the other girls fought with the door; meanwhile the flames rose higher and higher. Smoke began to fill the area closest to the stage, making it difficult to see and breathe. The temperature rose sharply as the Super Girls kicked, beat and shoulder charged the door, but it would not yield to their limited strength. By now the giant couldn't possibly have missed the commotion going on in the corner of the room and had fixed his sights in that direction. He thundered towards them, taking little time to traverse the great room with his huge legs and feet. Ripping the fiery curtain aside, he recoiled, mantle raised, mouth open, revealing rows of razor sharp teeth. Huddled closely together the Super Girls could only await their collective fate.

Then suddenly! the door gave way, sending them spilling onto the floor of a connecting room.

Presently they found it had not succumbed to their joint efforts but had been opened for them.

"Quickly, quickly," said Solo as she loomed over the heap of five, her slender hand grabbing any other she could find in the smoky half-light, flinging whoever was attached to safety.

"Solo!" exclaimed one of the 'flung', who turned out to be Wasp. "How did you…?"

"No time now Wasp, help me, won't you?" she coughed, as the smoke from the great room quickly began drifting in.

Whilst the doorway was being cleared of human clutter, the giant beast let out an angered roar on the other side of it. BB, who it now seemed could see through anything or anybody, kept the rest of the Super girls apprised of what was happening on the other side of the wall.

"Can you see Momo?" Willow asked.

"No not yet."

Solo took up Willow's hands in hers, gazing upon her with a serious expression.

"I'm going to get her, Willow."

"But Solo!" Willow protested.

"BB where's the giant now?" asked Solo with a tone of urgency in her voice.

"He's moving towards the far end."

"Willow, take the other girls to the back of the room, shelter in the left corner, leave this door open."

"Solo no!" Willow petitioned once again.

"Hush Willow, hurry now!"

Willow quickly organised the rest of the Super Girls and they sped through the dimly lit room as fast as they could. Back in the great room, Solo crept through the devastation and thick smoke. The meagre light left to navigate in, was rapidly being consumed by the ever-thickening veil. At the back of the hall a deep restless growl rang out. Solo made towards the sound and in doing so tripped on something, though what, she knew not.

"Ouch!" said a voice from within the darkness.

"Momo is that you?" Solo whispered.

"Yes it is," she answered, reappearing before her.

"What are you doing down there?"

"Staying low out of the smoke."

"What are you doing here?"

"I have a plan. but we must be quick."

"I'm listening." said Momo enthusiastically.

"First of all, I have to get back to the stage. Can you create a diversion for me?"

"Of course, what do you need me to do?"

"Reappear over near the door, it's been left open for you. Once you're near, attract the beast's attention. Then as soon as he makes towards you, run through it and don't stop until you've rejoined the others."

"Where are the others?"

"Safe and assembled in the far left corner of the next room," Solo reassured her.

"What about you?" asked Momo worriedly.

"Don't worry, trust me, I'll be fine."

As the beast stirred in the murky back drop, the two girls embraced for good luck and parted. Solo hurriedly retraced her footsteps back to the stage. There, she waited for Momo to reappear.

The smoke began to clear, funnelling up high into the roof and out of the shattered windows. As its shroud evaporated, Momo caught site of the enormous beast peering through what remained of its cover. Sticking to the plan, she began baiting it to keep its attention off Solo.

As soon as his eyes had locked onto hers, he set off, thundering across the debris strewn floor towards her. Following Solo's instructions to the letter, Momo ran the short distance to the doorway, now besieged by flames.

With the beast fast making ground, Momo took a deep breath and braced herself against the fiery mantle. Solo had precious little time to put her part of the plan into action and began frantically shouting and waving her arms above her head to refocus the beast's attention. Noticing her, it swiftly changed direction and began towards the stage on which she stood. The smoke retreated as the thundering mass approached, roaring and bellowing, mouth open, teeth bared. Solo held her position, preparing to put her faith in the power she had been gifted. As the giant closed in, the full extent of his ugliness clearly visible, she crossed her fingers, turned and leapt through the wall behind her. Meeting the floor on the other side with a bump, she picked herself up and instinctively began to run. Though there was little light available, Solo quickly located the other Super Girls and made frantically towards the corner they occupied. Only seconds had passed, when the very wall she had jumped through burst open with explosive force, bringing with it a cloud of dust and rubble.

Following the crash, came the strangled roar of the giant beast as it thudded slowly and pitifully to a halt amidst the destruction it had created.

Belly first, it sunk lower and lower to the ground, its head and neck briefly defying the fate of the rest of its bulk. Solo and the rest of the Super Girls watched wide eyed, as it swung from side to side like a pendulum. Slowly it lost momentum, until like a chimney stack being demolished, it came crashing down to earth. As its head bounced with the force of the impact, the jaws of its cavernous mouth flapped open, out of which shot the jewel in its belly, the fourth piece of the urn.

The room fell silent, save the sound of dust and debris settling all about.

"Is it dead?" asked Wasp hesitantly.

"I should think so," said Willow.

"It's quite sad really," said Momo in a melancholy tone.

"Sad!" exclaimed BB disbelievingly, "sad! it was about to kill us all Momo."

BB rolled her eyes and tutted.

"Anyway," she said boldly, "I'm going to fetch the piece of the urn."

With that she marched defiantly across the floor, leaving her footprints in the dust carpeting it. Stopping close to the beast's head she knelt down, reaching for the prize that lay only inches from its gaping mouth. Taking it in hand, BB stood up, readying to return to the group. Without any warning or sign, it let out a final, deafening roar. Dropping the piece of the urn, BB yelped, turned a milky white and sprinted back to the group.

"You said it was dead, Willow," BB panted accusatorially.

"I said I *thought* it was dead," she replied, making no effort to contain her amusement.

BB made a dismissive huffing sound and fell quiet.

Willow stretched out her arm in a gesture to usher one of the other Super Girls.

"A job for you perhaps the invisible Miss M?" she said to Momo with a knowing smile.

Momo slipped from view. Moments later the piece of the urn seemed as if it was floating in mid-air, until she rematerialized with it in hand.

"Now we have four pieces," she announced brightly.

"Only another three more and we're home."

"Indeed," said Willow, looking as if she was starting to believe it was an actual possibility.

CHAPTER II

Mongo

The Super Girls eventually found their way out of the giant beast's tomb, through a trap door in the floor. Walking backwards down an old, creaky, wooden ladder they entered a cold, dark, damp smelling cellar in which another door presented itself. After BB had checked there was nothing or nobody on the other side of it, the girls filed through. Crossing the threshold, they found themselves in a darkened passageway, though not anything cave-like, as they might reasonably have expected.

This particular passageway was more like something you would find in an old hotel. Its walls were panelled out in rich, dark, wooden planks about four feet in height, after which faded, parchment coloured wallpaper continued to the top of the arched shaped ceiling, some ten feet at the tip of the arc. Every twenty feet or so, an ornately fashioned wall lamp made a poor attempt at throwing its light into the path of the next one. There wasn't a great deal of room, just enough for the girls to walk in twos, Willow ever present at the head of the spear. For the most part they walked quietly along the meandering route, the little conversation between them, muffled in such close quarters. Time passed; still they walked on, until suddenly Wasp broke in.

"Shhh," she said in a voice a shade above a whisper.

"Do you hear that?"

"Hear what? I can't hear anything," dismissed BB.

"Oh do be quiet BB," Willow scorned.

"Listen carefully," said Wasp, her eyes narrowing as she strained to latch onto the sound.

"It's coming from behind us, but it's stopped now."

"Maybe because we have," suggested Roo.

"Yes Roo, perhaps you are right," agreed Willow.

"Let us continue on, if you hear it again Wasp, do say won't you."

The Super Girls pressed on through the corridor, following it through a series of bizarre twists and turns. Where it did not twist or turn, it rose and fell abruptly. In other spots the floor would fall away sharply across its width, making it almost impossible to stay upright on. Presently they arrived at a steep set of stairs leading downwards, until absence of light caused them to disappear entirely from view. The last of the sconce lights shone its feeble glow at the top, barely able to illuminate the first few flights. The Super girls halted at Willow's insistence.

After all they had faced so far, the stairs, or perhaps the darkness they led into seemed to have a most disconcerting effect upon them all.

Willow looked back at the rest of the group, her complexion turning pale.

"We've come this far," said Roo, tilting her brow, gesturing for Willow to face the darkness before them.

"Indeed we have," she replied.

Then turning, she took a deep breath and coursed down the stairs, allowing apprehension to delay her no longer.

Arriving at the bottom, the Super Girls were faced with a wooden door the width and height of the corridor itself. It was held in place by great, black, crudely fashioned hinges with a matching door knob. As they waited before it, Willow called BB to the front of the group so she might give an account of what lay on the other side.

There was a brief pause, for although BB had been gifted like most of the other girls with a special power, she had yet to master it fully.

"There's a room," she began, "with lots of windows."

Moving closer to the door, BB looked up.

"The whole room is made of windows, the ceiling too, and there are huge plants around the edges. I think it must be some kind of greenhouse or conservatory," she concluded.

"Is there anybody in there?" asked Willow, apprehensively.

"Not as far as I can see," BB replied, scanning the room one more time.

"I'll go check," volunteered Solo.

"Ok, but do be careful," Willow implored her.

Solo walked slowly towards the door, promptly bumping her nose on contact with it.

"Ouch!" she exclaimed, her expression equally as indignant as her tone of voice.

BB let out a muzzled laugh that could have easily passed as a snort.

Solo turned, the tautness of her features more than adequately describing her anger towards BB.

"Why don't I walk through you?" she declared, taking a step towards her, clearly intending to make good on the threat.

"Oh that's just creepy!" BB announced, seemingly in two minds whether to brace herself, or turn and run away.

"This, again!" said Roo despairingly, raising her hand to halt Solo's travel.

Solo paused, her expression changing from profound indignation to a similar degree of confusion.

"That's weird," she remarked, pressing her hand to her chest.

Roo looked at her questioningly, sharing her expression with the rest of the group.

"What is it?" asked Willow.

"I don't know," Solo replied confoundedly.

"I just felt a weird tingling sensation," she muttered.

"Probably just…"

"Quiet BB!" snapped Willow, pre-empting BB making any sarcastic comments intended to raise Solo's ire a second time.

"Don't mind her," she continued, gesturing to Solo to make another attempt.

Focussing her efforts, Solo clenched her fist tightly and moved towards the door once again.

Her second attempt successful, Willow called BB over to keep a vigil on her whilst she was in the room alone. A couple of taut minutes limped by before the door opened with Solo on the other side of it.

"All clear," she said tossing her head sideways, gesturing everyone in.

The girls cautiously filed by. Fanning out, their senses were overwhelmed with the colours and fragrances within. The huge plants BB had described, were just that. Standing about thirty feet high, they brushed the glazed, domed ceiling at the top of the circular room; the great expanse of glass supported by an ornate skeleton, fashioned from iron and painted white. The floor was made of large black and white diamond shaped tiles, gradually decreasing in size as they converged towards the centre. In the middle stood a fountain styled in the image of a cherub atop a huge stone shell. Etched upon it, a mottled turquoise trail, testament to the water that had once ran down it.

Four long, narrow greenhouse structures led off the rotunda at

90-degree intervals, each alive with a cornucopia of colour, texture and shape. Out of the corner of her eye Willow detected Momo taking a particular interest in the floor

"What's wrong Momo?" she asked, expressing her anxiety.

"Oh nothing, just making sure there aren't any beasts beneath us we should be avoiding," she replied with a mischievous grin.

At Willow's suggestion the girls split up, Momo and Roo in one direction, Solo, Angel and Wasp in another, she and BB in another still. Willow had carefully devised it so that the only two Super Girls yet to be gifted with a power, were flanked by at least one who had.

Whilst Roo explored one of the green houses with Momo, she confided in her that she didn't feel very super at all.

"What's it like Momo to be a real Super Girl?" she asked dejectedly.

"Whatever can you mean Roo?"

"You know, that thing you can do, blending into your surroundings so as to seem invisible."

"Oh that, well I hardly know, it's not like I really even see it," giggled Momo.

"Not like BB or Solo, now there's a gift."

"I'd settle for being able to walk and eat at the same time as things stand," said Roo, making no attempt to conceal her disappointment.

"Roo," said Momo taking up her hands, "if you hadn't broken the window in the village hall, we might none of us be here now. Besides, as we've progressed through the labyrinth, each of us has been gifted with a power as we've gone on.

I'm sure you'll get yours before we get out of here."

"You really think we'll get out of here?"

Momo looked at Roo squarely.

"We're the Super Girls, of course we will," she replied resolutely.

In one of the other glazed corridors, off the main rotunda, Solo, Angel and Wasp were foraging around for the fifth piece of the urn. Though they searched diligently for some time, they'd come up with nothing. Presently Willow and BB turned up.

"Found anything yet?" Willow asked, hopeful they'd had better fortune.

"No, not a thing" replied Solo.

"Perhaps we should go and see if Momo and Roo have had any luck."

The five girls made their way across the rotunda where the remaining two were busying themselves.

"Any luck here?" enquired Solo in a raised voice, sighting Momo and Roo at the far end of one of the greenhouses.

"Not yet," they hollered back in tandem.

Resuming their search, the girls began ferreting around in the giant, terracotta, flower pots and low walled, flower beds. Staying in the original groups Willow had suggested, they worked feverishly towards their goal. So zealous were they however, it hadn't occurred to any of them to look in perhaps the most obvious place for the 'prize'.

"I wonder what's going to happen in this room?" wondered Wasp aloud.

"Who knows?" replied Solo. "I know those plants really bother me though," she continued, casting her eyes towards the ceiling.

"Your dad knows about flowers and vegetables, doesn't he Angel?" asked Solo, anxious to further her knowledge of the giants looming menacingly overhead.

"Well he has a conservatory, not as big as this one obviously," she quickly pointed out.

"Do you recognise those things" she went on, pointing at the plants, a pinched expression demonstrating her distaste.

"Oh yes Solo, they're dinoaea muscipula."

"Dino, what?"

"dinoaea muscipula… venus fly traps."

"They're what?!" exclaimed Solo, narrowing her eyes.

"Venus fly traps," repeated Angel casually.

Solo paused for a moment, as if considering something.

"Just how tall are these plants meant to grow?" she discreetly enquired.

"Oh, about this big," gestured Angel with her hands, "not very big."

"What do they eat?" continued Solo with her line of enquiry.

"Flies, insects, things like that."

Taking Angel gently by the arm, she pulled her close. Looking skywards, Angel's eyes followed Solo's, as did Wasp's.

"What do you suppose these ones eat?" she asked, fixing her gaze upon Angel, searching her eyes for an answer.

There was another brief pause whilst Angel pondered.

"Oh," she uttered meekly, falling into Solo's line of thought. Then with subtle gestures made only with their heads and eyes, the three girls scurried away as inconspicuously as possible, collecting Roo and Momo on the way.

"What about the fountain?" exclaimed Willow excitedly, once all the girls were reassembled there.

"You read my mind," said BB, a distinctly puzzled expression remaining in the wake of her words.

Tearing away impulsively, BB dashed in the direction of it, readying to plunge her hand in.

"BB no!" bellowed Solo. BB froze as if she'd had a spell cast upon her. The room fell silent. Solo held her hand to her chest, sighing with relief.

"Just in time," she whispered to herself, nervously biting her bottom lip.

The rest of the girls stood perplexed, for nothing out of the ordinary seemed to be occurring.

Seconds later, a dull wrenching sound coming from behind the group, evidenced itself.

"Do not look behind you," said Willow quietly, "stay as still as you can." Whilst the girls kept their eyes fixed forwards, one of the giant plants passed slowly overhead, lowering its great stalk, resembling a giraffe at a watering hole.

Travelling further, it paused when reaching BB.

"Stay perfectly still BB, it won't see you if you don't move," cautioned Solo.

As the head of the plant drew nearer BB still, the full extent of its size could be appreciated. Its spiky, eye shaped head measured about five feet across, and though it had no features as such, it appeared to be grinning menacingly. BB stood with no more movement than a statue, and although she was ignorant of what was going on behind her, she knew staying that way was key to her survival. Thinking quickly, Solo threw her straw boater hat to BB's left. As it spun through the air, the plant lunged at it, effortlessly snapping it up in its giant mouth. The girls stood stunned, except Solo, who was far too offended that her hat, had effectively become plant food. She turned her head very slowly so that she might convey an idea to Momo without suffering the same fate as her hat.

"Pstttt."

"Yes," replied Momo in a feint whisper, standing as motionless as the others, even though she could have easily disappeared herself.

"If we can pass the word to Roo to create a distraction, do you think you can disappear yourself as you did in the auditorium?"

"Why, of course," whispered Momo.

"Ok then, get ready".

Momo remained, as the whisper passed from one Super Girl to the other, stopping when it reached Roo.

Out of the corner of her eye Momo saw Roo slowly and carefully remove her hat. Then just as Solo had done a few moments before, she threw it sideways. The fly trap immediately leapt after it, resembling a dog playing 'fetch'. Spitting out Solo's hat, it quickly closed its jaws tightly around Roo's. Recognising that it was one in the same it spat that out too. Solo took the opportunity to discreetly peek to her right, to see that, as planned, Momo had disappeared herself.

Leaning a little to one side to prove or disprove her theory, it was evident Momo was still there, just no longer visible.

"Pstttt" whispered Momo "I'm going to run to the left, when I rematerialize and the fly trap sees me, you and the others run in the opposite direction, alright."

"Ok" agreed Solo.

Solo passed the word down the line and waited.

It was a few taut seconds before the fly trap shot sideways, lashing out like a whip. Solo bundled the other girls in the opposite direction, grabbing BB on the way. Snapping wildly, the fly trap excited others of its kind, joining it in its pursuit of Momo. Taking refuge under the fountain's shell, Roo, Angel, BB and Wasp kept as still as they could to avoid detection. Willow situated herself in a place of safety, behind the stem of the fly trap that had first pursued BB. Meanwhile Momo kept them busy, disappearing and reappearing at random. Solo dashed across the floor to assist her. Seeing one of them coming directly towards her, she hastily disappeared through the glass, sending the fly trap head first into it after her. Shattering, it cascaded onto the unforgiving floor.

Lodged at the top however, one large piece remained, hanging precariously like a guillotine. As the huge plant began to recoil, it bumped and buffeted the sides of the window frame, causing the glass above to shake violently. Finally working loose, it coursed downwards, screeching like finger nails on a blackboard.

Meeting the stork, it severed clean its bloom. Solo re-entered the room, and seeing she had accidentally happened upon a way of slaying them, she set about doing it again. She and Momo worked feverishly until they had drastically reduced the numbers of the deadly foliage. The chaos abated, when suddenly those that remained, about half of them, inexplicably returned to the upright position they had first appeared in.

Solo looked at Momo, shrugging her shoulders.

"You think they've given up, Momo?"

"I really don't know," she replied, her eyes wide with bewilderment.

Willow appeared, stepping from behind one of the very plants that had been trying to devour two of her friends only moments before. Gingerly she crept over to them, all the time looking above and behind her. High up in the ceiling the predators remained, appearing as if they'd scarcely harm a fly, leave alone try to dine on twelve year old school girls. Continuing to approach, a broad smile crept over her face.

"Oh well done," she said clapping her hands together repeatedly, "you must have frightened them somewhat, they have completely given up."

The other four girls appeared from under the cover of the fountain, tentatively making their way towards the rest of the group. They were busy congratulating Momo and Solo when a curious gurgling sound interrupted them.

"What's that?" asked Roo, shooting her head around.

"It's coming from the fountain," said Wasp, pointing to it.

As they all looked on the noise grew louder.

Suddenly! from it, a thick black liquid resembling liquorice shot into the air, reaching almost to the top of the ceiling. Then, instead of cascading back down, it fanned out like a funnel, approximating the size of the fly trap's bloom. There for a moment it remained, frozen, like water from an outdoor tap on a frigid winter's day.

The Super Girls stood motionless, all with their eyes cast to the heavens. The brief silence that ensued gave way to a splintering, cracking type sound, as the black plume shattered into hundreds of pieces. As they slowly descended, a tuneless screeching sound filled the room.

"Those are bats," said Wasp pointing aloft with her mouth wide open.

"Yes," agreed Willow, "I cannot imagine they are particularly appetizing though," she continued, placing her hand under Wasp's lower jaw and lifting it gently back to a closed position.

Within seconds, the bats began coursing downwards at breath taking speed. The fly traps immediately sprang back to life, excited by the movements of the winged, black terror. The Super Girls scattered in every direction, taking advantage of any cover they could quickly find. The two species began working together, the bats kept the Super Girls moving, whilst the fly traps snapped and lunged wildly at them in travel. Roo, BB and Wasp had managed to reach the safety of the fountain, but the bats were coming in low and hard. Willow returned to her former refuge behind one of the stalks of the giant plants. It soon became clear however, mere hiding was not going to be enough to survive the 'black cloud' that had descended upon them. Out of the chaos Momo materialized next to Willow, giving the poor girl quite a start, as if she hadn't been startled enough.

"Any ideas?" she asked forlornly.

"Not really," replied Momo, as she clumsily fended off one of the creatures in question.

"There's just so many of them," she continued, looking at the churning black sea before them.

Beginning to fair less than well, Roo, BB and Wasp looked as if they were making a dash for one of the green houses, a dangerous move but necessary in the circumstances. Running in different directions the three girls each made for separate corridors. Wasp, surprisingly ran like a greyhound, disappearing through the entrance to one of the green houses in a flash. Roo too, fared well, only having to fight off a few winged assailants before disappearing into another. It was BB that seemed to be ill fated; tripping over, she fell face first on to the hard tile surface. Seconds later she was descended upon by bats from every direction. BB thought quickly however, rolling as if she was on fire, but there were just too many bats for this to be effective. The other girls knew if they tried to help her, they too would suffer a similar fate, or worse still, be snapped up by the giant fly traps.

With loyalty uppermost in her mind, Willow rushed out onto the floor from the relative safety of her refuge, Momo simply appeared there, followed quickly by Solo.

Immediately they too were besieged by bats. Struggling to fend them off, Solo and Willow stumbled around awkwardly, their arms flailing wildly about them. Momo's power was rendered useless on this occasion, for though she could make herself invisible, the bats could find her using sonar. Struggle as they may, the Super Girls were losing ground. When all hope seemed to have gone, the activity in the room inexplicably ceased. The bats and fly traps froze in a state of suspended animation, appearing as a three-dimensional picture. Momo reached for BB's hand, some were under a quilt of bats. Locating the requisite limb, she helped her to her feet. The four girls looked searchingly at each other, then around the room. Realising something of note had taken place, not least because the deafening noise had abated, Roo and Wasp appeared from their respective hiding places. With wide eyed, opened mouthed expressions, the two girls threaded their way through the 'living picture,' reuniting with the others.

"Wow!" exclaimed Wasp, aghast at the peculiar sight before them all.

"Wow indeed," remarked Willow.

"Where's Angel?" asked Roo.

"I thought she was with you?" said Willow.

"No," they chimed.

The silence continued, broken shortly thereafter by a muted swishing sound.

Turning to locate it, the Super Girls readied themselves for a shock, and they were in no small way disappointed.

"Emily Louise!" exclaimed Willow, instantly recognising the figure before her.

The girls instinctively huddled closer together at the sight of her.

"Where's our friend?" demanded Willow. Emily stayed mysteriously silent. Discomposed by this, Willow repeated herself.

Still Emily was unresponsive.

After some moments and without warning, she threw her arms high above her head. Startled by her strange behaviour the Super Girls stepped back in surprise.

Then tossing her head back, Emily finally broke her silence.

"Your work is done and now perhaps, it's time I sent you to the traps."

There was a momentary pause before the whole room sprang

back to life. The bats that had been suspended motionless in mid-air resumed their flight. Those that had come to rest on the floor peeled themselves off and sped upwards. Soon they circled the ceiling, filing one after the other into the open mouths of the giant fly traps. In a matter of seconds, the room was empty of them, save those that had perished in action.

Casting their eyes back to Emily, the Super Girls watched in disbelief as the image of her evaporated, leaving that of Angel's in its place.

"Angel?!" gasped Willow, her eyes narrowed, not believing what she had just witnessed.

"Is it really you?"

"Yes it's me," she assured her.

"How can we be sure?" Willow challenged her.

"Ask me something Emily couldn't possibly know the answer to?" suggested Angel.

Willow pondered for a moment, turning to confer with the rest of the Super Girls.

"Oh," said Wasp enthusiastically, "I know, I know. Who does Roo have a crush on?" she asked with an impish grin.

"Well," said Angel with a mischievous smile. "I would have to say Mr. Beckinsale."

The rest of the girls were quick to tease Roo, seeing that she had taken up his arm back at Horseforth and been very persuasive in matters of lunch. Roo blushed until crimson, quickly defending herself.

"I was simply trying to get us fed," she insisted.

The rest of the girls giggled.

"Ok," announced Willow, taking a step closer to Angel, "we believe you."

"How did you do that Angel?" asked BB, as she and the rest of the girls thronged around her.

"I don't know," she replied candidly, "the same way any of us do the things we can do, I imagine."

"We really are The Super Girls aren't we," said Wasp proudly, blushing bashfully.

"Angel, why don't you retrieve the fifth piece of the urn from the fountain?" suggested Willow.

"I will indeed," replied Angel, taking her turn to poke fun at the way Willow spoke.

As Angel claimed the fifth piece of the urn, BB had had to leave there, Wasp called her to a halt.

"Angel, wait," she said firmly, "I hear something".

"What is it Wasp?" asked Willow.

"It's the noise I heard in the corridor on the way here. It's the same noise that I've been hearing on and off since we entered the labyrinth. It's coming from behind the door we came in through."

Willow asked BB if she could see anything, but just as she began to focus her efforts, a small monkey appeared, walking straight through it.

"It's Mongo!" exclaimed Willow, her brow furrowing at the sight of the forlorn little creature approaching them.

In one of his tiny hands, Mongo was carrying a small green velvet purse, fastened together at the top by a gold cord.

When he was within a few yards of the girls, he timidly placed the purse on the floor before them. As he started to walk away he paused and turned, his little, dark, watery eyes met with Willow's, evidently trying to convey something to her.

With that, he scampered back from whence he came, leaving a profound silence in his wake.

"Open it then," said BB enthusiastically.

"Hush BB" scorned Solo, "don't you know who that was?"

"Anybody knows it was a monkey," replied BB tactlessly.

"No BB," said Solo raising her eyes, "that was Willow's Great-great uncle."

"Oh, oh!" exclaimed BB, putting her hand over her mouth, "you're right, I remember now."

"Funny how you always remember right at the end BB, isn't it," remarked Solo sarcastically.

Presently Willow knelt on the floor where lay the green velvet purse Mongo had left behind. Taking it in hand, she returned to a standing position and began to untie the gold chord securing it.

"I know what's inside," said BB excitedly.

"I bet you shake your presents before Christmas, don't you BB?" said Solo, rolling her eyes and shaking her head despairingly.

BB fell quiet; Willow returned to untying the purse.

Taking it from the bottom she held it upside down, her hand underneath the open end, ready to catch whatever resided within. Presently out fell a curved piece of porcelain like material, ornately decorated in similar colours as the urn.

The rest of the girls looked on.

"Looks like a piece of the handle," said Momo.

"It is," confirmed Willow, passing it around for the other girls to look at. "Angel why don't you get the piece in the fountain."

Hurrying over, she retrieved it without further incident.

"We have six, six pieces, one more and we're home!" she exclaimed excitedly.

Crouching on the floor, the girls lay all the fragments out, trying to fathom how they went together. Once achieved, they gave voice to their collective jubilation, giggling with abandon.

Flushed with excitement they prepared themselves to do battle for the last piece of the puzzle. Sitting in a circle, Willow suggested each of them make sure they have full command over the powers they had been gifted; starting with Momo, who on demand ceased to exist to the human eye. Next was BB, who described every piece of the urn exactly, even though they were randomly hidden behind the rest of the Super Girl's backs. Solo demonstrated her power by passing through the fountain and back again. Angel simply changed into the image of BB, quickly changing back at the others affectionate insistence. A task was set for Wasp in two parts. The first was that BB and Momo have a conversation in whispers the furthest distance from Wasp the building allowed, some three hundred feet or more. Wasp executed this task with complete ease, quipping, the two girls had no need to shout. The second task, was she read a note Willow had written in small print from the same distance. This she achieved with complete ease too.

Willow's E.S.P was harder to validate on account that it was a difficult thing to test. However, the Super Girls were unanimous in the opinion, Willow had always guided them, had never failed them, and had been able to do so from the very beginning of their journey. Then came Roo, who when it got to her turn, hung her head in shame.

"I don't have anything," she said apologetically.

"Darling Roo," said Willow in her less haughty 'mother of the group voice'.

"I know, I know," interjected Roo "you're going to tell me that had I not broken the window in the village hall we wouldn't be here now. Momo's already tried that one."

There was an awkward silence.

"No Roo, I wasn't going to say that, although it is true, you did save us, but not with a power, just your will. We are all singular in our gifts, but nothing without each other.

Look at Wasp and BB, they are our eyes and ears, Momo and Solo our defence, and Angel our disguise.

As for you Roo, you are our bravery, even without a power yet. It is you who is always first to go forward in any situation. Besides, your power will come, just when we need it most."

Roo lifted her head.

"Do you really think so?" she asked sorrowfully.

"Roo if you know anything of me, it is that I don't think, I know."

Willow embraced Roo, who had suffered great loss in her few short years of life but had gained so much by being one of the Super Girls.

"Spoken like a true leader," said Momo.

"Three cheers for our leader."

"Hip, hip, hooray, hip, hip, hooray, hip, hip, hooray."

Willow blushed.

"Where to now, oh great one?" asked BB with a grin.

Willow paused.

"Oh I think we should follow the monkey," she replied with a wry smile, at which BB sheepishly smiled back.

Carefully collecting up all six pieces of the urn, they left the room in search of the seventh.

CHAPTER 12

Emily's Return

It had been the first time the Super Girls had retraced their steps in the labyrinth. Perhaps naively then, they expected to find the same surroundings as those they had left behind them, but they were wrong. After proceeding back through the door that had led them into the greenhouse, they found themselves in a low, dark, narrow cave. Gone was the wooden, panelled corridor and the little oil lamps too dim and too far apart to be of any real use. Now all that lay before them was a cave, devoid of light, save Willow's tiny key ring torch Geoffrey had so fortunately given her. As usual she led the march, ever present on her mind what lay ahead.

In this surreal never world, they had gone from being seven ordinary girls to the stuff of fable. But was it all real? Perhaps thought Willow, it was all a dream and that tomorrow she would awaken, having only to fathom how vivid and detailed it all seemed. Dream or not she silently concluded, there was still one piece of the urn left to find. Continuing to trek through the dark void, she drew the girls to a halt.

"I see something," she said in a raised whisper.

"Can you make out what it is?" asked Momo, who was next down the line.

"No not really, I think it's just an opening."

"Why don't I go and have a look?"

"Ok," agreed Willow.

She made enough room for Momo to squeeze by, though space wasn't a luxury their present surroundings afforded much of. Once in position, Momo transformed into the colours and shapes of her background and disappeared. The rest of the girls waited anxiously for her safe return. In what seemed like a few minutes, she was back, remaining invisible until she reached Willow, lest she was seen or followed by anything or anyone.

"Well Momo, anything?" asked Willow.

"The cave opens out into a room just like the one we arrived in, torches on the walls and all. I didn't see anyone or anything more than that.

What do you think?" she asked Willow.

"I think we should all take a look."

Willow passed her instructions back along the line, and the girls started forwards once again. Within a few moments, they were in the room Momo had described.

"This is it alright," said Willow, feeling her skin grow cold as she spoke.

"The room we arrived in?" asked Angel.

"The very same, Angel."

"What shall we do now?" asked Roo, sounding strangely uneasy.

"Let's find the exact spot where we first met Emily Louise, we'll wait there.

"For what?"

"For Emily," replied Willow, her voice heavy with anticipation.

All seven of the girls walked over to where they remember standing when Emily first appeared before them.

Looking upon each other apprehensively in the half light, Willow suggested they hold hands and form a circle. Breaking the silence left to them, she began the Super Girl chant, knowing the others would soon join in.

"If we are to engage Emily in this very room," resumed Willow just above a whisper, we'll need to prepare. Momo, disappear yourself please, Solo, hide yourself in the walls, this will at least afford us some element of surprise."

Momo and Solo quickly embraced their friends, even Solo made her peace with BB, hugging her warmly. Then they were gone.

The ensuing moments felt like an eternity, everything was quiet, everyone was quiet, even BB. In the dim flickering light, Willow noticed a subtle change in Wasp's expression. With her heart rate beginning to accelerate she broke the uncomfortable silence.

"What is it Wasp, do you hear something?" she whispered.

"I do, I cannot say what though."

"It's coming from over there," Wasp continued, pointing to the exact spot where Emily Louise had first appeared.

Willow clasped hold of Roo's hand to her left and BB's to the right. Roo then took Wasp's hand, leaving BB to take hold of Angel's.

Giving a reassuring nod on both sides, the five girls readied themselves for the inevitable showdown with their nemesis. The noise Wasp had been hearing was now audible to all present in the room. Only a few more seconds passed, when just as before, a small, bright, orb evidenced itself. Its blinding glow quickly increased in size and intensity before drenching the entire chasm in light. As the girl's vision cleared, they stood once again before the menacing figure of Emily Louise. Their grip on each other's hands tightened at the mere sight of her, their hearts pounded, and their mouths ran dry. A taught silence followed thereafter.

"Well, well, well," sneered Emily sarcastically, "we meet again."

THE SUPER GIRL SEVEN

She paused, a thoughtful expression passed over her craggy face.

"But what's this I see?" she resumed, pointing one of her long-gnarled fingers at the group in a repeated stabbing motion.

"Only five of you? it seems that two of you little lambs have perished in my temple of torment." At this the room was filled with Emily's spiteful laughter.

After it had subsided, her expression altered, taking on a pensive, more thoughtful appearance. Observing this, Willow silently wondered if even the coldest of hearts may have some vestige of remorse, some seed of kindness.

Seemingly able to read Willow's mind, Emily spoke again.

"Well I confess I stand before you a little heavy of heart," she said, her expression somewhat softened.

"Then you are sorry for the loss of them?" enquired Willow naively.

"Oh yes," said Emily raising her voice as she leaned closer.

"I'm sorry that I won't get to torture them for all eternity as I will those of you who remain. Anyway, five it is," she said wearing a self-satisfied expression.

"So, do you have a preference for what animal you wish to be turned into to roam the labyrinth? please," she continued, "can you make it a little more imaginative than a frog, it's really so cliché, don't you think? and oh, before I forget, the monkey option's gone."

At this she cackled long and loud, suddenly stopping, her face turning to stone.

"Right!" she snapped "enough merriment for one century, who'll be first?"

The Super Girls gripped each other's hands tighter as they awaited their horrible fate.

"You!" she rasped, pointing to Wasp "you'll do, come here my pretty and choose the form you wish to take for all eternity."

"Don't do it Wasp," said Roo, her vice like grip preventing any ideas Wasp may have had of obeying Emily's demands.

"Ah," mocked Emily, "loyalty, how touching, and in the face of such impossible odds too."

"In the ugly face of such impossible odds," Roo replied scathingly.

Emily's eyes narrowed, for as ugly as she was, even she was not beyond vanity.

"Ah, I see we have our first volunteer. I suppose child with such a wilful spirit you will not come to me voluntarily?"

"I will not," said Roo defiantly.

"Very well then, let me see," said Emily in a smug tone.

"What rhymes with spider?"

She paused to think.

"Ah!" she exclaimed triumphantly after some moments, "I have it."

"Then casting her gaze exclusively at Roo, Emily began her spell, waving her arms about her excitedly.

"I gave her a choice, but she said I denied her, so after some thought, I turned her into a sp…."

"Stop!!!!" bellowed Roo, raising her hand up a split second before her fate was sealed.

Emily was suddenly thrust violently across the room, hitting the hard rock face before sliding down it like a rain drop on a pane of glass. Roo, still poised in the same position, looked sideways at Wasp who had been joined by Solo and Momo. Looking to her right, she caught sight of Willow, Angel and BB. All of them were stunned speechless.

Willow hurried over to Roo and threw her arms around her.

"I have my own power!" exclaimed Roo, tearful and dizzy with excitement.

"My very own Super Girl power!" she repeated, gleefully.

"Didn't I say you would," said Willow just as excitedly. The other girls rushed to congratulate Roo, but no sooner had they, Emily sprang to her feet.

Stunned, but no more than that, she flew at them, quite literally!

"Quickly Roo, do it again, do it again!" shouted Willow.

Covering the approaching image of Emily with the palm of her hand, Roo thrust her arm outwards to its full extent.

Emily was again repelled, this time less effectively owing to the speed with which she was travelling towards Roo.

Seeing that she had a worthy opponent however, Emily began to appear and disappear at random around the room. Bolts of lightning shot from her long sharp fingertips, sending chunks of the walls crashing to the ground. The larger of them made good hiding spots, the smaller ones, Roo sent hurtling back at her when she reappeared long enough for her to do so. The battle raged; Roo knew however, Emily would be the victor and subsequently their jailer if it went on for any length of time.

Remaining hidden behind an obliging boulder, she informed Momo and Angel of an idea she had, not altogether fool proof, but their best and only hope.

Seconds later Emily reappeared. Spotting her just in time, Roo elevated her off the floor and thrust her unceremoniously across the room once again.

"Now!" shouted Roo, *"go now!"*

Locating the very first tunnel they had originally ventured down, Angel and Momo grabbed the flaming torches off the wall and hurriedly shepherded the rest of the Super Girls into it. Hoping it still led to the abyss, they ran for their lives. Roo continued to battle with Emily, who had yet to notice all the other girls had gone. Knowing she was no real match for her, Roo blasted her across the room one more time and fled into the rabbit hole herself.

With no light to guide her, she fumbled blindly in the darkness as best she could. Emily would get there before her, of that Roo had no doubt. All she could hope was Momo and Angel remembered the plan she had hurriedly contrived. Breathlessly she continued on through the dark void until hearing the faint sound of voices in the distance.

Easing her pace, she neared a sliver of light which she hoped led to the chasm that had almost claimed Willow's life. As expected, Emily had arrived way ahead of her. Getting as close as she dare, Roo pressed herself hard against the wall to avoid detection, waiting for her moment.

"Well, well, well," tormented Emily, standing in front of the rest of the girls with the exception of Angel.

"It seems that you have developed some little party tricks of your own.

If I wasn't so evil, I'd put you all out of your misery by throwing you down there," she sneered, nodding in the direction of the fiery abyss.

"But alas, I am, and now that you don't have your friend with the magic hand to help you, it's truly time to meet your fate. Let's cast one spell over the lot of you and have done with this, shall we?"

Emily began her chant, then, as if sensing something was amiss, she paused.

"You," she said, stabbing her gnarled finger in Momo's direction.

"You're able to disappear and reappear at will. Why you could evade me for years in my little temple of torment, think of the fun we could have. At least you wouldn't be turned into a rat, a spider, or worse," she cackled.

177

There was a brief pause in which a thought seemed to be taking root in Emily's cunning mind.

"Yet you stay with your friends, how curious," she resumed with a confused expression.

"Perhaps you have mistaken me for another," said Momo.

Emily's face stiffened, as the image of Momo faded and was quickly replaced by that of Angel's.

An uncharacteristic look of disbelief beset Emily's features, for she knew she had been tricked and was about to find out, just how gravely.

"Now Momo, now!" shouted Angel to Momo, who had rematerialized in a crouched position at Emily's feet.

A look of horror spread across Emily's craggy features as she felt Momo clasp her hands around the backs of her legs. Nudging Emily's knees with her shoulder, the manoeuvre was complete.

In a world where magic and illusion prevailed, this simple tactic was enough to undermined Emily's centre of gravity, and thus, her supremacy. Desperately she waved her arms about her side trying to right herself but to no avail. Emily began to fall. Roo emerged from the refuge of the cave, rushing to the edge of the rock face and turning her hand towards their jailer. Thrusting it forwards, she summoned all the strength she had to keep her from zapping herself back on to the ledge on which she and the rest of the Super Girls where perched.

Emily's face was paralysed with fear, and though she tried to counter Roo's force, she twisted and writhed in vain. Roo's hand rocked back and forth as her adversary continued to struggle, though it was she for whom the battle was now slipping away. Piercing the molten rock, Emily let out an ear splitting, yet defiant scream. A brilliant glowed bathed the cavern, after which followed a deathly silence.

Emily was gone!

The Super Girls peered cautiously over the edge into the depths that had consumed her.

Half expecting her to miraculously rise from the lava and resume the role of their tormenter, they waited, but she did not return.

"Quickly," urged Willow, "let us go while we still can."

With a curious mix of exuberance and fear, the Super Girls retraced their steps through the narrow rabbit hole with only one thought present in their minds; returning home! A short while later they spilled out into the chamber they had first arrived in and began searching frantically for the seventh and last piece of the urn. Spreading throughout the room, it wasn't long before BB stumbled upon something.

"It's over here," she said, pointing to a large piece of rock that had broken away from the wall during Roo's battle with Emily. The girls gathered around, though they could see nothing, only the rock.

"It's in there," said BB as if no one believed her, "it's a big piece too," she added.

"But how ever, will we get it out?" asked Angel quizzically.

"Leave it to me," said Roo, proudly.

"What do you have in mind?" asked Willow.

"You'll see," she said with an assured wink.

"Now, everybody take cover in the mouth of the cave."

The rest of the girls did as Roo instructed and waited to see what she had conjured up.

After looking at the fragments and pieces of rock strewn about the floor, Roo hastened her way over to the others, standing with her back to the opening of the cave.

The rest of the Super Girls watched on as she stretched out her arm, obscuring her view of a boulder many yards away with the palm of her hand. Positioning it just so, she raised the boulder to head height, beckoning it towards her. Just before it hit her square in the jaw, she bought it to a sudden halt by turning her hand back outwards.

Summoning all her strength, she thrust the boulder towards the large rock containing the seventh piece of the urn. In a split second they'd made contact, the force of which sent a shower of fragments into the air. Roo quickly took cover in the mouth of the cave with the rest of the Super Girls. After the dust and debris had settled a little, they made quickly for the large boulder, now split perfectly in two, one half clearly displaying the last and by far the largest part of the urn. Freeing it carefully, they foraged around in their pockets for the other pieces, laying them out on the floor one by one. As they set to the task of reassembly, Wasp began to hear a familiar sound, hushing the group so she could locate it. Once there was quiet, she was soon able to tell from where it was originating, but not who or what was making it.

"It's coming from inside the cave," she said pointing to the one they had just vacated. The girls readied themselves for the possible re-emergence of Emily Louise, taking some comfort in the knowledge Roo now had a force with which to combat her. Whatever was making the noise couldn't be too far away, for soon all of them could hear it.

"Sounds like footsteps," said BB.

"What say you Wasp?" asked Willow, deeming her a more reliable judge.

"BB's right, it is footsteps, but who's?"

"They couldn't possibly be Emily's, could they?" said Angel, voicing the group's initial, and collective dread. The very thought of it sent a chill through the hearts of them all. Their fear was short lived however, for out of the darkness wandered Mongo. His appearance was met with a shared sigh of relief. Still though, the girls were wary, as the previously timid monkey made confidently towards them. Then in a blinding flash he disappeared, leaving in his place the image of Colonel Montgomery Forbes Hamilton. There was a stunned and uncomfortably long silence.

Breaking its grip, Willow ventured to speak, "are you my great-great uncle?" she asked nervously.

"I am the spirit of him my child."

"The spirit of my uncle?" questioned Willow, her expression conveying confusion.

"Yes my dear, the spirit."

"But how?" grappled Willow.

"Let me explain my dear, though perhaps you already know, but cannot except the depths to which evil will stoop.

I'm sure you are aware of the story of my impending engagement to Emily Louise and her disappointment when she found out I had been cut off from the family's wealth. What may still be in question, is whether or not she killed me, and the answer is, yes, she did.

Not content with this, she used her dark powers to transform me into the monkey you have seen and heard roaming the labyrinth.

She swore, rather than let my spirit rest it was to suffer for all eternity.

As you well know, the only way to destroy the labyrinth and free my spirit is to recover all seven pieces of the Urn of Sabu.

Obviously no mere mortal could achieve such a thing, but you and your friends have.

In all the decades my spirit has languished here, I was only ever able to retrieve the piece I turned over to you.

"Have you been following us uncle?" asked Willow.

"Yes my dear, I confess I have, however I could do little to help you.

Though I have witnessed all of you display great bravery, tenacity, tactical brilliance, and most importantly, complete loyalty to each other."

There was a silence as the two parties looked upon each other.

"Now it's time for us all to be free from this evil contrivance." continued the Colonel.

"I am more grateful than you will ever know, to every one of you, go well my children."

With that his image gradually faded until he had completely disappeared. Willow steeled herself against the sadness left in his wake, knowing the definitive truth about the Colonel's relationship with Emily and its bitter demise.

Taking a deep breath, she turned to the others.

"Let us go home, shall we," she said tearfully.

For a few seconds, Willow's words hung in the air as if unbelievable, like something you imagined you'd heard but couldn't possibly have.

Then as if the opportunity of returning home was in danger of disappearing forever, the girls quickly set about the task of reassembling the urn. It was very soon apparent however, that their efforts were rendered unnecessary. As they knelt on the debris strewn floor, a force appeared to be pulling the smaller pieces of the urn towards the much larger one. One by one it summoned all six of them from where they lay, seamlessly melding them back into their former position. Within moments it was in one piece again, emanating a strange mist from the opening at the top. The girls linked hands as a dense fog filled the cavernous chamber, the likes of which not even BB could see through.

CHAPTER 13

Home

It could have been seconds, minutes, hours or even days that the Super Girls had been imprisoned within the labyrinth; time seemed to have had no meaning in its confines. However, what greeted their eyes next had meaning enough for them all. They were home, or at least back at Horseforth Manor. They stood where they had left, at the turn of the stairs, just one short flight from the grand reception hall. The door leading to the labyrinth was gone, no vestige of it remained to help explain or support their story. Tired and much dishevelled they looked at each other in quiet disbelief before erupting into wild excitement. After their jubilation subsided, which took more than a moment, BB noticed the great, grandfather clock in the reception was about to strike three.

"Look!" she said pointing to it.

"It's still three o'clock."

"So?" said Roo quizzically.

"Well, how will we explain all of this to anybody if no time has passed, who's going to believe us?" BB whined.

"Well we have this," said Wasp, bending down to retrieve the urn, safely nestled in the corner of the stairway.

"Who brought it with them?" asked Willow.

There were blank faces all around; none of the girls had any memory of doing such a thing.

"Anyway, urn or not, we cannot tell any one of our adventure BB," said Willow.

"Why not?" she replied indignantly.

"Can you honestly imagine anyone believing it? besides, if they did, they would surely conclude we were all mad or witches, perhaps both, it's a preposterous idea."

"Well I'm going to tell people," said BB defiantly.

Willow turned to Roo and raised her eyebrows despairingly.

Though instead of an expression of despair, it was a signal to Roo; one which Roo understood and was happy to oblige. Placing her hand out in front of her to obscure BB's image, Roo began to raise her from the ground. BB's face expressed panic as she felt her feet leave the floor. The rest of the girls looked on as she rose higher and higher.

"Put me down Roo!" demanded BB, her face flushed with anger and embarrassment.

But still she continued upwards.

"This isn't funny Roo, put me down, tell her Willow," BB implored.

Willow stood defiant, bolt upright with her arms neatly folded across her chest.

"Promise to keep our secret BB," said Willow.

"I will not," she shot back defiantly.

"Very well," said Willow similarly.

Then turning to Roo, she gestured to her to continue. Roo raised her hand higher, until BB was a good eight feet off the ground.

"Excuse me," interjected Wasp meekly.

"One moment Wasp," replied Willow in a polite but dismissive way.

"Ok, ok!" conceded BB, who looked very odd and completely helpless just hanging in mid-air.

"I promise! I promise!" she growled, scarcely parting her lips to do so.

"Nothing crossed?" asked Willow with a self-satisfied grin on her face.

"Does it look like it?" snapped BB angrily.

"Very well then Roo, would you please."

"Must I?" quipped Roo, as she began to lower BB gently to the floor.

As she was so doing, the sound of footsteps evidenced themselves from the stairs above. Presently the familiar figures of Miss Worcester and Mr. Beckinsale came into view. The girls stood up straight, arms behind their backs. Unfortunately for BB however, Roo had not fully completed the task of bringing her back down to earth.

As Miss Worcester drew to a halt preparing to speak, there was a loud thud caused by BB completing the last couple of feet of her journey at the hands of gravity.

Everybody's head shot around; BB looked up, meeting Miss Worcester's stern gaze.

"Oh sorry Miss, I tripped on the rug, Miss."

She then quickly rejoined the rest of the group, scowling at Roo and Willow when opportunity allowed.

"Well?" said Miss Worcester, pausing to tuck her arms under her bosom, much the same as Miss Hoskins did when she was preparing for battle.

Scanning the group back and forth, eventually focusing on Willow, she resumed speaking.

"Well Miss Forbes Hamilton, judging by the state of you and

your…" she paused deliberately, "your friends, Mr. Beckinsale and I are in for quite a story."

Miss Worcester broke the ensuing silence.

"Well child, I'm waiting," she said impatiently.

"Oh yes Miss," replied Willow, nervously brushing the dirty hair from her brow.

"Well Miss, there was a dog."

"A dog?" repeated Miss Worcester with a sceptical frown.

"Yes Miss, a dog."

There was another awkward pause, though Miss Worchester's ire seemed to be in slight remission, subdued somewhat by her obvious curiosity.

"Well child… continue."

"Oh yes Miss, of course Miss. I came out to get some air, after not feeling well and saw a dog, out there," continued Willow, pointing out of the window to illustrate where she'd been standing.

"Well Miss it was limping, so I went into the grounds to try and catch it, so I could get it some help. One by one the other girls came looking for me. I suppose they were concerned for my wellbeing."

"What of the dog Miss Forbes Hamilton?" asked Miss Worcester, who as unlikely as it seemed, looked as if she was starting to believe Willow.

"Well Miss," Willow continued a little more animatedly, sensing this was the case.

"The dog ran into the old mine, so we went in after him, that is how we got so dirty and dishevelled Miss."

"Did you at least rescue the dog?" asked Miss Worcester, hoping for a positive conclusion to the yarn being spun her.

"No Miss, it ran out of the mine and into Mr. O'Keeffe's garden.

"Mr. O'Keeffe?" quizzed Miss Worcester with a frown.

"Yes Miss, he's the groundsman.

"I saw him put the dog into his Land Rover and drive off in the direction of the village, to the vets I imagine."

There was quiet, as Miss Worcester weighed the pros and cons of Willow's story. Mr. Beckinsale, (whose role in the entire exchange could have equally as well been discharged by a hat stand) stood with an inane sort of smile on his face. The silence became increasingly awkward as the seconds passed, until it was broken not before time by Wasp.

"We did find this though," she said innocently, reaching for the urn behind her and holding it aloft.

"We don't know what it is, but we thought perhaps…?"

Before Wasp had time to finish what she was saying, Mr. Beckinsale took the urn up in both hands with a curious expression of fear and elation on his face.

Composing himself he examined it carefully, taking out of his top pocket a special magnifying glass he held in his eye socket by means of squinting. Turning the vase carefully and mouthing what was inscribed upon it, he soon graduated to reading aloud.

"It cannot be?" he stammered "it isn't possible?"

"This is the urn! The Urn of Sabu!" he exclaimed loudly, indeed louder than Miss Worcester appreciated.

"I cannot believe it," he went on, and on, and on.

Then turning excitedly to the singularly unimpressed Miss Worcester, Mr. Beckinsale fumbled his grasp on the article.

To the horrified expressions of all present, except the ever-indifferent Miss Worcester, it travelled towards the unforgiving marble floor as if in slow motion. Any vestige of elation had completely vanished from Mr. Beckinsale's face as he watched on helplessly, the treasured artefact journey towards its certain demise. Roo, seeing the inevitable was going to happen, quickly intervened. Obscuring her view of it with her hand, she halted its travel, giving Mr. Beckinsale the time he otherwise wouldn't have had to recover it. Once achieved, Roo bought her hand up and about her face, pretending to sweep back her hair, albeit in an exaggerated fashion. Though her movement looked a little dramatic, she felt sure no one had noticed her affectation.

"Great catch Mr. Beckinsale," applauded Willow, encouraging the other girls to join in, further diverting suspicion. Miss Worcester cast a scowl over them, at which the applause immediately ceased.

"Where did you say you found this?" asked Mr. Beckinsale, when he eventually composed himself.

"In the entrance to the old disused coal mine Sir," said Roo, electing herself spokeswoman for the group, since she was the most convincing liar, Willow a poor runner up at best.

"How odd," he muttered, looking completely baffled.

"No matter," he continued, brushing off the mystery of its former whereabouts so he could indulge in the jubilation of it being recovered.

"This is the best day of my life, it's a curator's dream," he beamed.

"Miss Worcester, aren't these the most divine group of girls you have ever had under your charge?" gushed Mr Beckinsale.

They are certainly the grubbiest," she replied disdainfully, clearly nowhere near as impressed as he was.

"No," he said with an inane smile tattooed on his face, "I must respectfully protest, they truly are super girls.

At this remark, the girls all looked at each other with a grin.

"You are to be commended," Mr. Beckinsale went on, "perhaps a piece in the local newspaper," he said excitedly, at which Willow's expression turned to one of horror.

"I shall talk to the trustees, but for now I really must go."

Taking his leave of the girls and Miss Worcester in that order, he left, clutching the urn as if it were a new born baby, twittering merrily away to himself in travel.

"Now," said Miss Worcester with a stony expression, "what's the real story?"

The girl's faces fell, especially Willow's.

"Oh never mind, go and wait for the bus the lot of you," she sighed resignedly.

It didn't take long for it to arrive, completing the journey to the house, this time without issue. Everybody filed on including the Super Girls, conspicuous by the dishevelled state they were in. "Blimey," said the driver as they stepped aboard "did you girls go for a visit or help out with the renovations?"

"Very funny," retorted Willow, attempting to straighten her blazer and dust herself off. The other pupils seemed to need to comment on the Super Girls' appearance too, when they ran the gauntlet between them and the back seats. As the bus trundled down the long drive, passed the gatehouse and onto the main road, Camilla Spencer turned in her seat.

Camilla was fourteen years old and in the fourth year at the Stanley.

Although she resembled Willow in many ways, with her long blonde hair and tall, narrow silhouette, she was nowhere near as pretty and refined. In the arena of family fortune, she fell short too; although from a wealthy background, her parents were not nearly as moneyed as Willow's. For these reasons and perhaps others best known to herself, she did not like Willow, or any of the other Super Girls, whom she deemed guilty by association.

"Oh look at the lovely Miss Forbes Hamilton in her casual collection," she sarcastically jibed.

"What's the matter Hamilton, the family business not doing so well?" Along with her two side kicks, Devina Prior Palmer and Petula Perkins, the three girls continued poking fun at Willow and the other Super Girls. A short while into their journey, the bus squealed to a halt in the steep dip between West Denton and Sutton Althorpe.

Miss Worcester made her way to the front to ask the driver the reason for their delay.

"Old farmer Braithwaite's shepherding his flock to the top field, we'll be here for a good ten minutes," he informed her.

It was an unusually nice day for autumn, sunny, bright and still quite warm for late afternoon. Given the conditions, Miss Worcester seized the opportunity to step off the bus and spend time outside, away from children.

Camilla and company utilised her absence to be even more obnoxious, enlisting the support of spotty, little, teenage mutants, Jeremy Watkins and Nigel Sumner.

"Oi Hamilton," piped up Jeremy under his mop of black, greasy hair, "thanks for taking the blame for that fire extinguisher incident."

The gang of five laughed heartily, with no one to police their behaviour. Willow didn't much mind the unwelcome attention, but Wasp was less equipped to deal with it.

"Oi," said Nigel, referring to Wasp, "where's your bumble bee costume?"

"It's in the wash Nigel," said Jeremy, "ready for the next fancy-dress party."

They punctuated the end of their jibes by laughing loudly, encouraging other kids on the bus to join in, who were more than happy to oblige. Finally Roo stood up, paused for a moment and then went to raise her hand, which the other Super Girls knew meant certain discovery.

Willow shot from her seat taking up Roo's wrist, looking at her squarely in the eyes.

"Ignore them," she said firmly, "they must not know."

Roo relaxed her arm "you're right, you're right," she agreed, returning with Willow to a seated position.

"What was you gonna do Oz, zap us with your special powers?" said Nigel, much to the merriment of the other kids.

"Be careful!" shouted a voice from the front, which turned out to belong to Adam Tierney.

"The tall one's a witch."

"They all must be then," said Nigel.

BB had had enough; she stood up from her seat to address the assembled tormenters.

"Camilla," she began with a sarcastic smile on her face.

"Shall I tell everyone on the bus that you stuffed your training bra with tissue paper today because you knew there would be older boys on the trip... oops," said BB coyly, pressing her finger to her mouth, "I just did."

In seconds, Camilla's face was aflame with embarrassment, and though she stammered for words, none came out. Seeking the only refuge available, she stormed off the bus.

The Super Girls broke into laughter, whilst BB lined up her next victim.

"Jeremy," she announced.

"You don't have anything on me Barnes," he said smugly.

"Oh but I do Jeremy... I do," she assured him.

Jeremy's face drained, betraying a weak spot, which BB was about to expose with the very breath she was drawing.

"We were just joking with you," appealed Jeremy nervously, turning towards the front of the bus.

"Oh like the fire extinguisher was just a joke too, Jeremy?" scorned BB.

There was a silence in which Jeremy thought he had avoided BB's wrath, but not so.

"Where was I?" asked BB rhetorically, "oh yes. Jeremy was late for school today everybody."

"So, is that it?" Nigel chipped in, defending his cohort.

"No," said BB "if only it were. The thing is, in his haste to get to school, Jeremy put on his sister's knickers by mistake, or maybe it wasn't a mistake?" BB posed the question.

"So our friend Jeremy has spent the whole day in girl's underwear," BB announced.

Jeremy's hands folded around his face, his head dropped into his lap as if it were too greater weight to hold upon his shoulders; one could almost feel the heat he was generating.

The tormenter became buried under an avalanche of ridicule as the bus resounded with laughter.

"As for you Nigel Sumner," scalded BB.

"Don't tell them Bailey, please," he pleaded, waving his hands in front of him. *"Please!"* he repeated, looking sorrowfully at her, his face wracked with fear.

BB paused, "very well," she said mercifully.

"But in future Nigel, be nice to my friends, or I will embarrass you in ways you couldn't even imagine," she warned, before reclaiming her seat.

Solo looked at BB, nudging her shoulder with hers.

"Oh well done Super Girl," she said with a broad grin on her face.

"Yes, excellent work BB," agreed Willow.

"Yes," chimed Wasp, "thank you for sticking up for me," she added shyly.

"So was any of that true?" asked Willow, voicing the thoughts of the other Super Girls.

"Well," said BB "the part about Camilla and Jeremy was."

"And the other bit about Nigel?" asked Wasp.

"Oh I was just bluffing there." said BB with a grin, "but it seemed to do the trick, don't you think?"

The journey resumed with hardly a word spoken from any of the bus's occupants the rest of the way.

In only a few minutes they were back at school, the Super Girls never imagining they'd be as glad to see it as they were. Upon their arrival they were greeted by Mr. Bradley, who hastily took Miss Worcester aside, speaking to her in hushed tones behind one of the pillars that supported the main entrance. It was impossible to hear what they were speaking of. Impossible for mere mortals perhaps, but decidedly easy for the likes of Wasp, who was completely privy to the conversation.

"What are they talking about?" asked Willow in hushed tones.

"There's been some trouble in the library with Miss Hoskins," she replied.

"Mrs. Hill is frightened half out of her wits, the library looks like a demolition site and Miss Hoskins has disappeared altogether."

"Where on earth to?" asked Willow.

"Mrs. Hill insists she turned into a witch and vanished before her very eyes."

The girls all looked at each other with similar expressions of apprehension etched on their faces.

Just then Mr. Bradley broke in.

"Ok, if you could just all listen," he began. "As it's Halloween weekend, I'm going to let you go home half an hour early today.

The school is now closed until Monday," he concluded.

"We should take a look in the library," insisted Willow.

The rest of the girls were in agreement. So as Miss Worcester and Mr. Bradley re-entered the building in the front, the Super Girls raced around the back. As they walked through the desolate corridors, the sound of their footsteps echoed eerily. Rounding the corner that led to the library, they noticed its big, wooden door ajar, as if some one had left in a hurry. Willow bought her slender hands to rest on its handle, opening it carefully, she was reminded once again of entering the labyrinth. Swinging it wide open, it creaked and whined as usual, there any similarities to a normal library visit ended. Strewn about the floor were books of every size and description. Some of the shelves had met a similar fate, odd, given the size and the weight of them. Where windows were broken, the curtains ebbed and flowed with the gentle breeze they were exposed to.

"Upon my word!" exclaimed Willow, *"what on earth has gone on here?!"*

The girls ventured further into the chaos, having to carefully navigate their way through the debris obscuring the highly polished, wooden floor. Once they reached the back of the room, Wasp's attention was suddenly stolen.

"Quickly! Miss Worcester and Mrs. Hill are coming," she whispered loudly.

"Hide!" said Willow, "Miss Worchester's sure to tell us to leave if she finds us in here."

Taking cover, they awaited their arrival.

"Are you sure you'll be alright here on your own Mrs Hill?" Miss Worcester could be heard saying.

"Yes I'll be fine now, thank you," she replied resolutely.

With that Miss Worcester left, her footsteps becoming fainter the further away she got.

Once Mrs. Hill had re-established herself in the room, the Super Girls came out from their hiding places.

"Good grief!" she exclaimed, pressing her hand against her chest, you scared me half to death. What are you doing here, I thought Mr. Bradley sent everybody home?"

"We came to bring back our library books Miss," said Roo thinking quickly.

"Do you really think they'll be missed," said Mrs. Hill casting her eyes over the destruction.

"We could help you put things back," said Wasp.

"You're very kind my dear but where would we start?"

Mrs. Hill fell silent, suddenly noticing how dishevelled all the girls were.

"How on earth did you get into that state?" she enquired.

"Well you'd never believe it Miss," BB blurted enthusiastically.

"It's a long story Miss," Willow interjected, cutting BB off before she said too much.

"What time was it when you saw Miss Hoskins turn into a witch and disappear Mrs. Hill?" Willow continued.

"You mean you actually believe me?"

"Yes Miss, of course Miss," replied Willow earnestly.

"What about the rest of you girls?"

"Yes Miss," they chorused.

"Very well, I will tell you. At about three, I put my head up to look at the clock and saw Miss Hoskins standing motionless before me.

As the moments passed she gradually became enveloped in a glow of light.

When it had engulfed her completely, it expanded at an alarming rate, filling the room in one explosive surge. That's when everything went tumbling over, the windows burst forth and all hell let loose. After I regained my sight, for I was momentarily blinded, there she was standing before me."

"Was her appearance altered?" asked Willow.

"Oh yes my dear," said Mrs. Hill emphatically, "she looked much aged and gnarled, but that wasn't the worst of it. No, it was the expression on her face I'll never forget."

"Can you describe it Miss?"

Clearly unsettled, Mrs. Hill took a few moments to compose herself. After a brief silence she resumed.

"It was evil dear, pure evil."

"Then what Miss?"

"Then she cackled in the most spine chilling manner and simply vanished."

A silence fell between the two parties.

The Super Girls looked at each other searchingly but were soon interrupted.

"You didn't come here against the wishes of Mr. Bradley to return library books, did you? Besides, how is it you know what I thought I saw? no one would have told you such a thing."

"No Miss," conceded Willow.

"Then why?" asked Mrs. Hill, making careful study of the faces before her.

Willow cast her eye over the rest of the group to gain their approval, and once she knew she had it, she took a deep breath.

"Miss... can you keep a secret?"

The end ... or maybe not?